SENIOR PROM

SENIOR PROM

BY

Rosamond du Jardin

J. B. LIPPINCOTT COMPANY
PHILADELPHIA
NEW YORK

CONTENTS

To Scott du Jardin, with love

SENIOR PROM

1

PRELUDE TO A PARTY

NEITHER Marcy Rhodes nor her brother Ken was actually eating dinner at home on New Year's Eve. Liz Kendall had invited as many of the old crowd as were available to a dinner party before the country club dance. And, of course, Marcy and Ken were going.

"Not that I'd suspect you were eating out!" their mother, Lila, exclaimed in mock exasperation as she moved about briskly, broiling steaks and mixing salad for herself and her husband, George, who was due home any minute.

The Rhodes' kitchen was a cheerful place, bright with checked gingham curtains and scarlet pots of ivy on the window sills, but it wasn't particularly large. Twice Mom had caught herself on the verge of tripping over Ken's size-twelve feet as he sat sprawled comfortably at the table. And Marcy kept hopping up from her seat opposite him and getting in her mother's way in order to add to the impressive sandwich she was building.

Her glance at Mom was warm as she slid into her seat with an air of finality and put a slice of bread on top of the conglomeration of meat and cheese and pickle and mayonnaise and lettuce she had accumulated. "Now, Mom," she said, "you really wouldn't expect us to last clear through till seven-thirty on empty stomachs, would you?"

"We'd starve," Ken announced starkly, preparing to bite into his sandwich. It was a twin of his sister's, except that it was cemented together with peanut butter instead of salad dressing.

"We couldn't have that," their mother said. "Knowing what bottomless pits you both are, I'm sure you'd need some sort of little snack to tide you over. But I should think those messes would spoil your appetites entirely."

"Mine's delicious," Marcy objected, nibbling.

And Ken admonished in a pained tone, "Kindly refrain from referring to this mess as a mess, Madam, or you may offend my delicate sensibilities."

It was on a burst of laughter that the back door opened and Dad came in. A thin, amiable-looking man, he beamed at his family through glasses so fogged by the change of temperature from outdoors to indoors that he couldn't see a thing. "Sounds as if you're having fun," he said.

There was a chorus of affectionate greetings. As soon as he'd wiped off his glasses, Mom lifted her face for his customary kiss.

"Steak for dinner," she told him. "I hope you're hungry."

"That aroma would make anybody hungry." Her husband sniffed appreciatively. "Are we celebrating New Year's a day early?"

"Mom figured," Marcy teased, "that steak for two was

cheaper than for four. So she took advantage of our eating out."

"Of course," Mom went along with the gag. "Have to cut corners some way after all we spent for Christmas."

Dad frowned, having forgotten momentarily why Marcy and Ken weren't eating at home. Then his face cleared. "That's right," he nodded. "You're going to Liz's before the dance." As his glance fell on Marcy, however, his frown returned. "What kind of a getup is that?" he asked.

A silk scarf only partially concealed Marcy's dark pin curls and she was wearing a plaid duster and her red lamb's-wool scuffs. Moreover there was a dab of medicated cream on her chin where she had feared a pimple just might dare to show its ugly head.

"Don't worry." She grinned at her father. "I won't go like this. I took my shower early so there wouldn't be such a run on the bathroom later. Stinky-poo here," she wagged her head toward Ken, "has to have lots of time to make himself beautiful and smooth-shaven and sweet-smelling—"

"How," her brother cut in, "would you like to have the soggy remains of my sandwich in your lovely little puss?"

At his threatening gesture, Marcy clasped her hands in supplication. "I take it back," she said hastily. "You're bigger than I am."

"Smarter, too," Ken drawled. "And much better-looking. And haven't you noticed my winning personality?"

"We-ell—" Marcy managed to instill a note of profound doubt in the single long-drawn-out syllable.

She and Ken laughed then. And a warm little glow kindled in Marcy, fed by their laughter and the good-natured banter that masked the solid reality of their understanding and affection. It had always been so with her and Ken, ever since they were children. No matter how much they squabbled and argued and failed to see eye-to-eye on an issue, it didn't shake the firm foundation of their relationship. And now that they were grown up, with Marcy in her final year of high school and Ken away at college most of the time, nothing had changed between them. The affection and understanding were, if anything, deeper than ever. They still disagreed on occasion, but each respected the other's viewpoint, his right to think things out and arrive at his own conclusions. Theirs was a good relationship, Marcy thought fleetingly. She was lucky to have such a brother—not that she'd ever dream of telling him so. A slight smile curved her lips at the very notion.

"What's so funny?" Ken demanded. Having finished his sandwich, he poured himself another glass of milk from the bottle on the table between them.

"I was just thinking," Marcy murmured dreamily, "how wonderful it'll be after Wednesday, when you're back at college and I can take a shower when I like without having to consider you."

Even as she said the words she felt a little nip of loneliness, a sort of forewarning of how much she would actually miss Ken when he'd gone. Having him home for two whole weeks had only served to set the old happy pattern so firmly again that his departure would leave a ragged hole in it, just as had been left when he went away to college for the first time last fall. Oh, darn! she thought. Why did I have to remember how soon he's leaving?

"Is that so?" Ken said. "Well, don't think it won't be a pleasant change for me to get back to the fraternity house where I don't have to eat with females in pin curls and bathrobes."

And neither of us mean a word of it, Marcy thought. Rising, she gathered her duster about her regally. "Okay," she tossed back as she departed. "I'll just leave, since I'm obviously not appreciated here."

As she passed Ken she deliberately stepped on his outstretched foot, then rushed for her room, laughing gleefully.

"You'd better run," Ken threatened. "I'll attend to you later!"

In the privacy of her bedroom, Marcy proceeded to embark upon the pleasant ritual of getting ready for the big evening ahead. Steve wouldn't call for her for almost an hour, so she had plenty of time. Still, dressing for New Year's Eve wasn't a thing you could rush. As she began freeing her soft dark hair from its bobby-pin prison, Marcy's thoughts dwelt on Steve Judson. Day after tomorrow he would be leaving for Carveth College, along with Ken, and she'd be left behind. Somehow though, fond as she was of Steve, the thought of his going didn't carry in its wake the sheer panicky misery she had felt last fall, when he left for the first time. Then it had seemed as though she couldn't bear it. He had been her mainstay, the one she counted on.

But time had taught her that she could get along with-

out him. Oh, it had been hard at first. Marcy still remembered the painful loneliness, the bitter sense of not
belonging, that had chilled her during those first weeks
after Steve's departure. His letters hadn't helped much.
She had tried to build up a pretense of not caring to
date, of not liking any of the boys in her class at school.
But hiding behind such obvious untruths hadn't been
easy. She couldn't even fool herself. And she had begun
to wallow in self-pity, all the more corroding for being
kept locked up inside of her.

What a little dope I was, Marcy reflected, brushing
her hair till all the set stiffness went out of it and it fell
softly about her pensive face.

But she wasn't really looking at her reflection. She was
remembering how things had seemed to pile up on her
when her mother, a registered nurse of years' standing,
had decided to go back to work at the hospital, where
help was needed so badly. Then, in addition to her
school work, Marcy had had to take on extra household
responsibilities as well. But, at least, there had been less
time for brooding. And, actually, she had snapped out
of her unhappy self-absorption rather quickly, rescued
by her own common sense and some down-to-earth advice from her brother.

Seems to me, Marcy thought ruefully, Ken's always
straightening me out. Wonder if I'll ever reach a point
where I don't need it?

She felt so kindly toward her brother at the moment
that, hearing his plaintive howl from the bathroom that
he'd forgotten to bring in a towel, she padded cheerfully
out to the linen closet in bare feet and ruffled crinoline

petticoat to get him one. Hanging it on the doorknob, she called above the rush and splash of the shower, "There you are. And don't say I never did anything for you."

"You're a good kid," Ken yelled back appreciatively.

Before Marcy had finished dressing, Ken left to pick up Rosemary Ames. Hearing the front door slam behind him, Marcy felt a small prick of pity for Rosemary. Ken and she used to date a lot, but since he had gone to Carveth, he was much more interested in a girl he'd met there, Lee Creighton. Rosemary knew about Lee, of course, and she herself dated other boys. But Marcy suspected she still carried a torch for Ken, whereas his feeling for her was strictly of the good-old-friend variety. He was only going out with her tonight because Lee's home was hundreds of miles away.

Would Steve and she ever be like that, Marcy wondered? She felt a sharp ache at the thought.

She stood back from the full-length mirror on her closet door for a last reassuring look at herself. Her deep green velvet and net formal, ballerina short and full, couldn't have been more becoming. Her hair had turned out well, too, Marcy thought gratefully, and the blemish she'd worried over hadn't developed at all. Her skin glowed creamy-dark and clear above the vivid color of her dress, and her brown eyes shone with pleasurable anticipation. Certainly Steve should be impressed with her tonight.

She was dabbing a touch of Christmas perfume behind her ears when the door opened and her mother entered.

"About ready?" Mom asked. "We just heard Steve's car on the drive. Dad's letting him in." She got a good look at Marcy then and said, her eyes lighting in the immemorial manner of mothers, "You look wonderful, dear."

"You're prejudiced," Marcy accused, giving her a little hug. "You look wonderful yourself."

Mom had changed into a soft blue dinner dress, with a becoming scooped neckline. Her gray-frosted blond hair curled upward from her ears and gave an animated youthful look to her pleasant features.

"Why, thanks," she said, obviously appreciative of the compliment. "This dress isn't new, goodness knows, but I've always liked it. We're going over to the Martins' for some bridge—they're having a couple of tables—and then we'll all be out at the country club later. Your father," she added ruefully, "and most of his contemporaries, for that matter, will only take just so much dancing."

"Yes, I know," Marcy murmured. "We'll see you there, then."

Her mother nodded. "Have fun, honey."

"Oh, I will," Marcy promised, catching up her velvet coat with the draped collar that could be pulled up over her head into a warm hood. "Steve and I always have fun."

From downstairs she could hear the murmur of masculine voices talking with the ease of long acquaintance. She hurried down the hall toward the stairway lightly, her feet scarcely seeming to touch the carpeting, her thoughts winging ahead. She was so anxious to see

Steve's face lifted as she approached, to watch the light of approval break in his eyes, to know that he was as eager as she to have the evening begin. If only, she thought, it could last and last forever, so that Wednesday would never come and Steve wouldn't have to go back to college at all.

2

OLD ACQUAINTANCE

S TEVE stood with Marcy's father in the lower hall and, just as she had hoped, he turned at the sound of her footsteps and looked up at her. It was funny how the scene took her back. For a moment she was a scared fifteen again, coming downstairs in her first formal, a white one, her heart hammering and her palms damp. Dating had been so new to her then and Steve had seemed more Ken's friend than anyone who could really be interested in her. She had felt tongue-tied and unsure and the prospect of the school dance looming ahead had filled her with a sense of terror rather than expectation. Two years ago that had been, yet Marcy made the round trip back to the present between heartbeats. The smile she gave Steve was radiant and his look as appreciative as she had dreamed.

Of course, he didn't stammer and gulp, as that two-year-younger Steve had done. His, "Well, well! You're looking very sharp tonight," was spoken in the man-of-the-world manner a few months at college had made seem so natural to him.

"Thanks." Marcy's own voice was poised and confident. "You, too."

Steve handed her the florist's box he was holding. "I hope these go with your dress all right."

Thanking him, Marcy lifted out a cluster of pale yellow roses. "Oh, Steve, they're lovely!" She held them against her velvet bodice, so he could see the effect. "I'm going to keep them in the box till we get to Liz's, though, so my coat won't crush them."

Her mother had come downstairs behind Marcy and they all stood and talked for a few minutes before Marcy and Steve said good night and started to leave.

"Take it easy, Steve," Marcy's father warned. "There are so many crazy drivers on the road New Year's Eve."

"I know," Steve answered. "I'll watch it."

He didn't seem to mind the advice, but Marcy felt a twinge of resentment as they walked toward the car. Couldn't Dad realize they were no longer children? And Steve had never been reckless.

As if he had caught the echo of her thinking, Steve said, "You should have heard the lecture my dad gave me along with the car keys tonight. I guess it's hard for them to believe we're grown up."

"I guess so," Marcy agreed, "but it makes me mad just the same."

Steve chuckled. "As you get older, you don't mind so much. I used to take it a lot harder than I do now." He looked up at the sky. "It's quite a night, isn't it?"

Marcy nodded, looking up, too. The stars were crystal bright against the black immensity, and the slight snow that had fallen earlier lay along the edges of the walks and in the hollows around the bushes like ruffles of silver lace.

"It looks exactly the way New Year's Eve should look," she said, as Steve helped her into the car.

"I ordered it special," he confided, sliding under the wheel beside her. "Four million stars, I specified, and just a touch of snow for trimming and not too cold. Personally, I'd have liked a little more snow, but we can't have everybody skidding around and getting stuck in drifts after all the parties and dances, just because I have a yen for a white New Year's."

"True," Marcy agreed. "You do take everything into consideration, don't you?"

"Always thinking." Steve tapped his forehead with one finger as he started the car.

Liz lived so near, they might as well have walked, except that they'd need the car for getting out to the club later. Steve said as much and added appreciatively, "It's really pretty decent of all our parents, letting us use the cars."

Marcy nodded. "I guess they're all going out to the club with the Drakes."

"And you know how the Drakes happen to have their car available?" Steve chuckled. "Because their kids are married."

Marcy smiled, wondering aloud, "Do you suppose our folks look forward to the day when they can call their cars their own again?"

"Could be," Steve said, "but I doubt it."

Marcy doubted it, too. Parents were funny that way.

Steve said, "A cousin of mine down in Kentucky just got married. He's only a few months older than I. And you should have heard my folks sound off on how foolish he was to marry so young."

"Well, don't you think so, too?" Marcy asked.

"Yeah, sure," Steve agreed. "But things get awfully complicated sometimes. I mean—well, there's college and then the army waiting to grab you. Or if you get your service out of the way first, you're an old man before you finish your education. It makes marriage seem so darned far in the future."

"I know," Marcy said. Life wasn't simple these days, especially for young men. She'd heard Ken kick the whole proposition around often enough so that she could feel a real sympathy for Steve's uncertainties.

"Sometimes," he said, "a guy just gets to thinking, 'The heck with it!' Maybe that's how my cousin Don felt." He swung the car in to the curb before the Kendalls' brightly lighted house and shrugged, grinning at Marcy. "Oh, well, New Year's Eve is no time for settling weighty problems."

"Let's just have fun!" Marcy exclaimed.

And that was exactly what they did.

Considering how the old crowd had scattered, Liz had managed to get a good many of them together again. There were boys home from college, a few in uniform, coupled with girls they'd dated last year when they were all still in high school. Everyone was very gay; talk and laughter billowed in waves through the Kendalls' recreation room, and yet Marcy was vaguely troubled by the feeling that this was different from the parties they used to have.

Sitting with a tray of food on her knees, participating

in all the fun, Marcy yet tried to put a mental finger on the difference. Was the talk too incessant, the laughter too ready? Were they all trying too hard to capture an old effortless ease, a lost closeness? They were the same people, doing familiar things, yet it was as though each of them were trying to squeeze back into an outgrown garment that no longer quite fitted.

We aren't the same as we were last year, Marcy thought. We're trying to pretend to be and it isn't quite coming off.

Her glance sought Liz, fair and lovely in pale blue, across the gaily decorated room. She was talking animatedly with her date, Bill Weaver, home from school in Texas. Yet Marcy knew Liz no longer cared much about Bill. She greatly preferred Hank Novak, who was still in high school and whom she dated a lot. Bill had invited Liz to the country club dance, but she wouldn't suffer a bit when he went back to college. Right this minute Hank might be haunting her thoughts.

Marcy's speculative glance traveled on around the room. Why, it could be that way with most of the couples here tonight! Any of the boys might have girls at college they preferred to their present company. Even Steve. Marcy knew there was a girl at Carveth named Thea Cunningham whom he liked quite well. Maybe, she thought, better than me.

She wasn't going to brood about it, though. After all, Steve wasn't the only boy in her life. The thought of Rick Whitney immediately popped into her mind. Rick was the tall, quiet boy she had dated most often since Steve had been away. Their friendship was warm and real. And there were others at school quite capable of stirring her interest. Bruce Douglas, for one, although he hadn't asked her for a date yet. But he will, Marcy thought confidently.

"Why," Steve's voice broke into her reflections, "are you looking so starry-eyed?"

"Was I?" Marcy hedged, feeling a little guilty.

It was a relief to hear Liz's voice just then, suggesting that if everyone had finished eating, they ought to be taking off for the club. In the enthusiastic murmur of agreement that arose, the clatter of dishes and trays being stacked on the table, Marcy had no trouble at all in changing the subject.

The country club dance, long a New Year's Eve tradition in Westfield, was, as usual, very well attended. And, also as usual, the crowd was a mixed one, composed of teen-agers, young marrieds, parents and a sprinkling of sprightly grandparents. On New Year's Eve seventeen-year-olds waltzed happily with men three times their age and beaming college men guided gray-haired matrons through the intricacies of the samba. Of course, after a few such dances, the various age groups gravitated unfailingly to their kind. But the atmosphere of camaraderie and high spirits that knit them all together prevailed throughout the evening.

Marcy danced with her father while Steve danced with his mother. Afterwards, Marcy told Steve with a little giggle, "Dad didn't actually say 'That's that!' when it was over, but his manner implied it. Parents are cute, aren't they?"

Steve, who was mopping his perspiring forehead, agreed, "Cute, but harder to lead than girl friends."

"They get such a kick out of dances like this, though," Marcy said. "I like them, too, occasionally. Why," she wondered aloud, "do some kids seem to feel that anyone over twenty-five is automatically disqualified from being any fun?"

"Search me," Steve shrugged. "I have nothing against older people."

"After all," Marcy went on, "it's silly to act as though middle age is some sort of rare disease. It's going to happen to all of us."

"Sure is," Steve agreed, "gruesome as the idea seems."

"What's more gruesome," Marcy said thoughtfully, "is when you get really old and haven't any family left to care about you. That's when it's awfully rough."

Old Mr. Tuttle, one of her mother's patients at the hospital, was in exactly that situation. He'd been laid up for months with a broken leg and, if it hadn't been for Marcy stopping in fairly often to play chess with him, he'd have had no visitors at all. Marcy's throat thickened a little with pity, remembering Mr. Tuttle. He was such a dear.

"I have a hunch," Steve said grinning down at her, "you're thinking of my ancient rival, Mr. Tuttle. Not very flattering, is it, with me right here?"

"Sorry," Marcy murmured, "but you know how fascinating these older men can be."

"Still," Steve kidded, "if I didn't have anyone under seventy to cope with, it wouldn't be so bad. It's the younger guys you chase around with that worry me."

"I'll bet," Marcy said. "In between dates with all those gorgeous college women, you must brood about it."

The music began again and Steve held out his arms. As Marcy moved into them and felt the old familiar magic take over, she wished the dance never had to end. . . .

By the time Marcy and Steve got home it was quite late. Most of the older crowd had left the club soon after all the horn blowing and balloon popping and friendly jollity of the midnight celebration. But the younger element lingered until the last strains of "Good night, Sweetheart" died away.

As Steve pulled up on the Rhodes' drive and shut off the ignition, his arm went along the back of the seat and Marcy leaned her head comfortably against it.

"So it's a brand new year," Steve said.

Marcy nodded. In a way, New Year's Eve seemed rather a sad time. Maybe that was why people always made such a big, gay thing of it, with parties and noise and all, so that they could push aside the shadow of its sadness. A time of endings, of looking back and totaling up, a period to the year just past.

When she put her thought into words, Steve objected, "Yeah, but it's also a time of beginnings, of looking ahead and wondering what's going to happen next."

"That's right," Marcy agreed. "Endings *and* beginnings."

"I'm glad that's settled." Steve pulled her closer.

But Marcy felt like talking. Somehow it seemed they hadn't had much chance for it during the holidays. There had been so much going on all the time. She'd even squeezed in a couple of dates with Rick Whitney, because it hadn't seemed fair to simply drop him while Steve was home and then expect to pick up their friendship again once the holidays were over. Rather to her surprise, she felt a stir of excited interest at the thought of Rick. He wasn't as handsome as Steve, but there was a quiet charm about his tall lankiness and slow smile. And Marcy and he were amazingly congenial. They shared a love of poetry and both liked to ride horseback and write for the school paper.

"I have a feeling," Steve said, "That your thoughts are far away. Do you realize how soon I'll be leaving?"

"Yes, I do," Marcy said sadly. "And we've hardly had a chance to talk at all while you've been home. Somehow—I don't feel as if I know you as well as I used to, Steve."

"You know me well enough." He chuckled. "A few months at college haven't made a new man of me."

"But both of us have changed some," Marcy persisted, "because everything that happens to people changes them a little. And lots of things have happened to us."

"Look," Steve coaxed, "must we get all involved in a deep philosophical discussion right now?"

"No, of course not." Marcy had to smile at his tone. "But I was just thinking how much more sensible I am about your leaving this time than I was last fall. Then I was all upset. It seemed like the end of the world. And I was jealous in advance of every girl you might date, even when I was telling you to go ahead, that it was the only sensible thing to do."

"But you don't feel that way any longer?" he asked.

"Well, no," Marcy said frankly. "Oh, I don't mean I'm not sorry you're going, Steve, or that I won't miss you. But now I know I can enjoy myself with other people and still have fun, even with you away. And I want it to be like that for you, too." She was still fond of Steve. She knew that. But there were others she liked, too. Am I dreadfully fickle, Marcy asked herself, or do all girls my age feel so uncertain and confused?

"This isn't," Steve's low tone was suddenly serious, "a velvet glove brush-off?"

Affection for him surged up warmly in Marcy. "Oh, Steve, of course not!" she told him. "It's just that I was such a prize dope last fall, I thought you'd be glad to know I've got more sense now."

He chuckled, drawing her close, and Marcy made no effort to pull away. "Yeah, now that you put it that way, I guess I am," he admitted. "I want you to miss me, just as I'll miss you. But I'd hate to think of you brooding all alone and being miserable the way you were at first."

"Any more than you expect to brood all alone and be miserable," Marcy added.

"Well—yes," Steve agreed, and they laughed together just before he kissed her.

3

NEW JOB

MARCY sat in study hall, her history book open on the desk before her, and tried hard to keep her thoughts from wandering. American history was one of her favorite subjects and usually she made the most of her time during this final period, since the more work she did at school, the less she'd have to take home. But this was the first day of classes after the long, exciting Christmas vacation and everyone was finding it hard to get back into the groove. More eyes in the room were fixed dreamily on space, or staring out the windows, than were bent on textbooks. Even Miss McCollum, the journalism teacher, who had charge of this study hall, was staring frowningly off above the heads of the class, her mind quite apparently on other matters.

Sighing, Marcy managed to focus her full attention on the chapter concerning the causes of the Civil War, which had been assigned for tomorrow. And by concentrating doggedly she had become so involved in the events leading up to the shelling of Fort Sumpter that the shrill sound of the bell terminating the period brought her back to the present with a start. All about her relieved people were shutting books and getting to their feet, happy that the first day after vacation had been lived through. Marcy felt happy, too, as she gathered her books together and joined the crowd surging toward the doorway.

Rick Whitney, rather engagingly awkward, ambled up beside her. His slow smile had a secret quality, as though he were keeping something exciting to himself.

"Meet me out in front when you get your things?" he asked. "I've got news for you."

"Okay," Marcy nodded. Rick walked her home once in a while, although he always had to tear back to school to catch the bus afterward, since he lived a few miles out in the country. She suggested, "Can't you tell me now and not keep me in suspense?"

Rick shook his close-cropped head mysteriously. "Nope."

They were passing Miss McCollum's desk when the teacher said, "Marcy, I want to talk to you. Can you wait a few minutes?"

"Why—" Marcy's voice showed her surprise, "of course."

But she wondered as she stopped and stood there, what she had done. No one had been studying very seriously. Why should she be singled out for a reprimand?

Rick said, "See you out front," and Marcy nodded.

Miss McCollum gathered her papers together with maddening deliberation as the room cleared. Not until they were quite alone did she begin talking. And with her first words, Marcy realized with relief that she hadn't been detained for a calling-down.

"Marcy," the teacher said earnestly, "I have quite a

problem and I hope you can help me. You know Dick Whalen, of course?" At Marcy's nod, she went on, "What you may not have heard is that the Whalens are moving rather suddenly and that Dick won't be coming back here to school. Which means that he's had to resign from the staff of the paper and that the *Breeze* now has no feature editor."

"I hadn't heard about that," Marcy admitted in surprise.

Miss McCollum nodded and again the faint frown Marcy had noticed earlier wrinkled her forehead. No wonder she was upset, Marcy thought. The journalism teacher was advisor for the staff of the Westfield *Breeze* and vitally concerned in the paper's publication. She said, "Feature editor is such an important job, it must be filled right away."

Marcy could see that, still she wondered why Miss McCollum was unburdening herself to her. Marcy liked to write and she had done some work on the *Breeze* as a reporter, so she knew a little about the mechanics of the publication. Was Miss McCollum going to ask her for suggestions as to who would be competent to serve in Dick's place? Marcy had already begun to bend her thoughts toward this problem when the teacher spoke again. And her next words made Marcy stare at her blankly, lips parting in utter surprise.

"I wondered," Miss McCollum said earnestly, "whether you'd take on the job?"

"M-me?" Marcy gulped, quite forgetting her grammar.

The teacher's smile lit her face warmly. "You'd be very good, Marcy. I can tell that from the work you've already done for the paper. You have a knack with words and such original ideas."

"Why—thanks," Marcy murmured. The teacher's words of praise made her feel wonderful, still feature editor was such a vital job. "I've only done a little reporting," she said.

Miss McCollum told her, "That's all Dick had done until last fall when he took on the staff job. And all of us would help you in any way we could. I'm sure you'd get your bearings in a short while."

Deep down inside, Marcy thrilled to the idea. It was a great compliment to be asked to serve on the *Breeze*'s staff, even if she would be filling in only for the rest of the year. Her face must have shown how much the idea appealed to her, because Miss McCollum reached out to give her hand a friendly, encouraging little pat.

"You will consider it seriously, won't you? I don't expect you to make up your mind this minute."

Marcy nodded. "Oh, I will think about it. I appreciate being asked—only—I wonder if I could really handle it."

"I'm not worried about that," the teacher assured her, "or I wouldn't be asking you. And your grades are high enough, so I'm sure you could spare the time from your studies."

Marcy said, "I have quite a lot to do at home, too, Miss McCollum. You see, my mother works. She's a nurse at the hospital."

"Oh?" the teacher's voice sounded a little less confident. "I didn't know about that and, of course, I wouldn't want to interfere with any other responsibilities you may have. But I do hope you can do it, Marcy."

"So do I," Marcy said impulsively. "I'll talk to my parents about it right away. When will you have to know?"

"By the end of the week," Miss McCollum told her.

"I'll think about it seriously," Marcy promised, "and let you know before then."

The corridor was almost empty and she moved along it and down the stairs to her locker without conscious volition. Her feet followed the familiar route instinctively, her hands reached in and got her coat and angora ear muffs and mittens. She donned them automatically and made her way to the school's front entrance without once taking her thoughts off the exciting proposal Miss McCollum had made to her.

It wasn't until Rick Whitney's dry voice demanded, "Hey, what are you doing, sleepwalking?" that Marcy plopped back into the present and realized exactly where she was.

She gave him an apologetic look. "I guess so. Gee, I'm sorry I kept you waiting so long, but—"

He broke in before she could explain what had happened, "That's okay. Come on." His hand on her arm propelled her briskly through the gray slushy day. There was no mistaking the controlled excitement in his voice, his movements.

Marcy remembered then that he had spoken of having something to tell her. The talk with Miss McCollum had pushed her curiosity about Rick's news out of her mind. But Marcy felt it flare up again as he guided her around the corner toward the back of the school.

"Where are we going?" she queried. "I live that-a-way, remember?"

"I remember," Rick said mysteriously. "Don't ask so many questions. This is a surprise."

They were cutting across the school's graveled parking lot now and suddenly Marcy felt herself brought to a dramatic halt beside a light green Ford of ancient vintage and very little distinction. But Rick stood there with such a glow of pride lighting his features that Marcy guessed the truth at once.

"Oh, Rick!" she exclaimed. "Is it yours?"

He nodded, beaming. "Every dent and scratch and rattle belongs to me." His delighted voice didn't go with the depreciating words at all.

"It's just wonderful," Marcy said enthusiastically. "I didn't realize you were even thinking of buying a car."

"Well, Dad wouldn't let me till I could pay cash," Rick admitted. "And he also insisted I find one with a dependable motor, no matter how the outside was. I agreed with him on that. So I've been saving my money and looking. And I worked on the snowplow for the county during the holidays and the pay was good. Then I stumbled on this," he laid a loving hand on a badly dented green fender, "and it's got the sweetest motor a guy could want." His eyes sought Marcy's hopefully. "You don't figure the body's as important as what's under the hood, do you?"

"Oh, of course not!" Marcy said positively. "And

anyway it looks fine to me. I'm so glad for you, Rick."

"Me, too," Rick agreed. He opened the door, which only stuck a little, and helped Marcy in with elaborate courtliness. Going around to the opposite side, he slid in under the wheel. "Now I won't be a slave to that darned school bus any more," he told her, grinning. "That's been the only drawback about living in the country. But with a car of my own—" he left it at that and started the motor proudly. "Listen to her purr."

"Nice," Marcy approved. Although it sounded to her exactly like any other motor.

Most of the way home Rick pointed out the admirable features of his new acquisition. The brakes, Marcy agreed, were excellent. There was nothing wrong with the upholstery that some new seat covers wouldn't hide, as soon as Rick could afford them. And the gas mileage, as attested by him, was almost miraculous.

It wasn't until they were within a block of Marcy's house that Rick thought to ask why Miss McCollum had detained her. When Marcy had explained, Rick's enthusiasm over the journalism teacher's suggestion matched her own.

"Gee, that's swell," he said sincerely. "I can't think of anyone who'd make a better feature editor than you."

"I don't know, though," Marcy said. "There's a lot of hard work involved. I'd have to stay late at school a couple or three times a week. Actually, though, that's not the thing that bothers me. I just wonder if I could handle it."

"Sure you could," Rick said staunchly. "Miss McCollum ought to know. And, as she says, the rest of the staff would help you. And, gee, if there was any way I could, I'd help, too."

"Would you, Rick?" Marcy asked. "You write a lot better than I do." C417479

"Nuts!" Rick's tone was derisive. "But I'd sure do anything I could, like helping proofread and run material down for you, mechanical stuff like that."

"That would be wonderful," Marcy said gratefully. "*If* I decide to try it, that is. Of course, I'll have to talk it over with my parents. I can't let Mom down with things at home just so I can work on the paper."

"I'll bet they'll tell you to go ahead," Rick insisted. "Especially if you want to do it—and you do, don't you?"

Marcy nodded. She did want to very much. Ever since Miss McCollum had broached the idea, it had become more and more appealing to her. Marcy Rhodes, Feature Editor. She could almost see the words printed on the *Breeze*'s masthead. Still, she wasn't going to let her hopes rise too high till she'd had a chance to talk with her parents.

When Rick had let her out at her door and had driven off, Marcy went up the walk and into the quiet, empty house. This was the angle she disliked most about Mom's working, this bleak period between the time when she got home from school and her parents' return. Not that there wasn't enough work to do to fill up the time. And today Marcy's thoughts were so excitingly occupied, she didn't even feel lonely.

By the time she heard the car pull into the garage,

Marcy had dinner ready and the table set. It was a good dinner, too, the beef patties broiled just right and the vegetables nicely seasoned. She had even baked an apple pie, the frozen variety, of course, but none the less tasty for that reason.

"You," her father beamed at her as they lingered over dessert, "are getting to be almost as good a cook as your mother."

"I think it's wonderful," Mom told her, "how you've taken hold here at home. It's such a big help to me."

Basking in their appreciative approval, Marcy felt she'd never find a better moment to broach the subject she'd had such a struggle to keep to herself even this long. She started out with the slightly breathless announcement, "You'll never guess what happened after study hall today!" And, within half an hour, everything was settled. Marcy honestly didn't think she had misled her parents. She answered their questions frankly. It would mean extra work, she admitted, but it would be work she'd like doing. And she wouldn't let her studies suffer, or do any less to help her mother at home. "I'll manage my time better," she said earnestly. "I know I can do it."

She was so persuasive that Lila and George caught fire from her enthusiasm and grew as excited over the whole thing as Marcy herself. She had often thought they were very satisfactory parents and now she felt more sure of it than ever.

They were just getting up from the table when the phone rang and Marcy dashed off to answer it.

"Hi, Marce," Liz's familiar voice came along the wire.

"Sorry," Marcy tried unsuccessfully to keep the lilt out of her tone, "but you'll have to be more respectful. This is the new feature editor of the Westfield *Breeze* speaking."

4

HAPPY ENCOUNTER

MARCY was a little late for her next regular Thursday evening chess game with Mr. Tuttle. He was waiting patiently in his wheel chair, the board set up on a small table, his bright old eyes fixed on the doorway as she came through it. His lined face beneath crisp white hair lit at sight of her.

"Thought you'd stood me up for some of those young squirts that are always after you," he told her.

Marcy smiled affectionately at the indomitable old man as she answered, "Now, you know I wouldn't do that!" Slipping out of her coat she explained, "What really delayed me was that I had to go back to school after dinner and help proofread the paper. We go to press tomorrow and it's always a madhouse just before that."

"Didn't know you worked on the school paper," Mr. Tuttle said, with his usual lively interest in her doings.

"That's right!" Marcy exclaimed. "I haven't seen you since it happened." She proceeded to tell him about her exciting new job and how well she liked it. "But it's a lot of work," she added. "I thought I was busy before, but I didn't even know the meaning of the word."

"Feature editor, eh?" Mr. Tuttle eyed her proudly.

"That makes you one of those big wheels, I reckon."

"Oh, no," Marcy shook her head. "I'm not that important."

Mr. Tuttle nodded firmly. "A genuine bona fide big wheel, right here in my room, ready to play chess with me. Seems like we ought to do something special to celebrate the honor."

Marcy knew when she was being kidded, no matter how straight Mr. Tuttle kept his face. "I'll beat you," she said. "That'll be special enough, after the way you usually trim me. Come on now, let's get going."

"All right," Mr. Tuttle whacked the arms of his chair with enthusiasm. "This'll be the battle of the century."

They went at their game with pleasurable intensity. No matter how busy she was, Marcy thought, she wasn't going to let anything stop her visits to Mr. Tuttle. He had practically no other company. His wife had died years before and he had no children, no relatives that he ever mentioned. Before long now, as soon as a housekeeper could be found to look out for his needs, he would be leaving the hospital and going home. But Marcy was determined to continue their association. She was so fond of him and, despite his sometimes crotchety air of independence, she knew how much he counted on her for friendship. Loneliness could be so dreadful when one was old and had outlived or lost touch with most of one's contemporaries.

Their game reached stalemate, just a few minutes before time for the gong to sound ending visiting hours. "A draw," Marcy said philosophically. "Well, at least that's closer than I usually come to winning."

"You were pretty sharp," Mr. Tuttle commended. "Your game's getting much better."

"I hope yours doesn't," Marcy said drily. "Anyway, it was fun."

The old man nodded. "Sure was." He hesitated a moment, then, his slightly apprehensive gaze on her face, he said, "Maybe it's going to be too hard for you to fit our weekly game into your schedule, now that you're an editor."

"Don't worry," Marcy said with mock fierceness. "I'll keep coming back till I can really win instead of just managing a stalemate."

The grin he gave her was so relieved that she felt tears sting her eyelids and her own smile grow a bit tremulous as she said good night. Walking down the echoing corridor toward the stairs, she blew her nose and took a hasty swipe at her eyes with her handkerchief.

And just then she heard footsteps striding up beside her and Bruce Douglas' voice saying, "Not getting a cold, I hope?"

Marcy denied it, feeling her heart quicken, as it invariably seemed to at sight of the blond, exceedingly attractive young man, who was always so friendly and agreeable when they ran into each other by accident, but who hadn't, as yet, asked her for a date. Bruce's father was a doctor and Bruce occasionally stopped in at the hospital to see him. This was by no means the first time Marcy had encountered him in the corridor. Sometimes she gave him a lift home, if she happened to have the family car parked outside. Sometimes he did as much for her. Once he had even suggested they have a soda at the Sweet Shop on their way. Now expectation quickened in Marcy as she smiled up at Bruce.

"There must be something around here that you're allergic to," he said, "or it wouldn't give you the sniffles."

"No sniffles," Marcy denied. "No allergy."

"Good," Bruce said. "I was afraid it might be me."

"That I was allergic to?" Marcy laughed softly, as befitted a hospital hallway.

"Sure," Bruce nodded. "I read about something like that in the paper a while back. A couple got a divorce because the wife was allergic to the husband. He made her break out in hives."

"Oh, fine!" Marcy exclaimed.

"Of course, I'm not your husband," Bruce pursued the idea absurdly, "so it's not quite the same thing, is it?"

Marcy shook her head. "Not at all. Besides, I don't have a single hive."

"Good," Bruce said. "What I'm mainly interested in, is whether you have a car."

"Right out in the parking lot," Marcy told him. "You want a lift?"

"No, I wasn't hinting," he shook his head. "I've got my car out there, too. I was going to offer you a lift."

"I'm sorry," Marcy said. "Thanks anyway." She tried to keep the disappointment she felt from sounding through her tone. Darn it, if she'd walked the few blocks to the hospital and figured on taking a cab home, she could have accepted Bruce's invitation. But no, she'd had to drive, just because the car was available.

"I'm sorry, too." Bruce held the heavy door open for her and walked beside her down the broad stone steps that led to the street. To Marcy's delight, he sounded as though he really meant it. "Better luck next time."

She nodded and they turned into the graveled parking lot, where the big lights overhead made the night seem almost as bright as day. Bruce stopped beside a small, obviously new, yellow convertible. He said, "I was going to give you a ride in my Christmas present."

Marcy's eyes widened in astonishment. "Really, Bruce?" she exclaimed. "You mean—that's yours?"

He nodded. "From my folks. It isn't just for Christmas, though. It's my graduation gift, too, and my next birthday. This is the only present I'm going to get this year—but it's enough."

"How wonderful!" Marcy exclaimed, touching a shining chrome door handle delicately. "You're lucky."

And, of course, because the situation was so similar, like a scene from a rerun movie, she thought of the recent afternoon when Rick had marched her out to the school lot to see his new-old car, the faded green one with its dents and scratches. Boys with cars—how alike they all were, Marcy thought indulgently. But there was a world of difference between these two cars. Still, Rick had worked hard to pay for his while Bruce's was a gift.

"Tell you what," Bruce said, struck by a sudden idea. "How about you driving home and me trailing you? Then we could head on back to the Sweet Shop for a bite to eat. You have to see how the bus rides, at least."

"Okay," Marcy agreed enthusiastically. "It's a deal."

The trip home was accomplished in a few minutes. She put the car in the garage and detoured into the house for just a moment to explain to her parents where she was going.

"With whom?" Dad asked, frowning at Bruce's unfamiliar name.

"You've heard me speak of him," Marcy reminded. "He's Dr. Douglas' son."

"Oh," Dad said, nodding, his disapproval draining away.

And Mom smiled, reminding, "Just don't forget it's a school night, honey. That old alarm rings awfully early."

"I won't," Marcy promised. "I'll be home within an hour. We're only going to the Sweet Shop."

Bruce, who had waited in the convertible, held the door wide for her. "You didn't have trouble getting out again?"

Marcy shook her head, settling luxuriously deep in the cushions of the wide seat. "Not a bit. They just reminded me it was a school night in the most tactful way."

Bruce chuckled. "I'll get you home early. Growing girls need their sleep."

"So do growing boys," Marcy reminded.

"You sound like my father," Bruce said, "only your voice is softer."

He drove a couple of blocks, then turned, not to the right as Marcy expected, but left, away from the main part of town. Set for the other turn, Marcy was thrown off balance and slid over involuntarily against Bruce's shoulder. "Hey, you're going the wrong way."

"Who says?" Bruce asked. "Wouldn't you like a hamburger instead of a soda? I'm starved."

Marcy suddenly discovered that she was starved, too. The Lighthouse, where Bruce was apparently heading, was only a couple of miles out of town. It wouldn't take long to get there. "Besides," Bruce went on reasonably, "if we just drove to the Sweet Shop, you wouldn't have much idea what a great little bus this is. She'll do a hundred and twenty easily."

"A hundred and twenty?" Marcy said, appalled, straightening up. "That's crazy!"

"Oh, I don't mean I've tried it," Bruce said. "But that's what the salesman told us. Of course, my father's already laid down the law about what he'll do if I go over the speed limit. So you needn't worry."

"I wasn't worried," Marcy denied. "I figured you had too much sense to actually drive that way."

"Then relax again," Bruce said. "I liked the feel of you leaning against my shoulder. It was real cozy."

Warm, hated color stained Marcy's face at Bruce's teasing. She was glad it was too dark in the car for him to see. She did relax a little, resting her head against the back of the seat. And when the car's motion swung her a little closer to him, she rather liked the sensation, too.

In no time at all, they reached the Lighthouse. As they made their way through the brightly lit restaurant, Marcy saw several familiar faces and smiled and spoke. Bruce, too, greeted people he knew. But he made no move to join any of the other couples. Instead, his hand under Marcy's elbow propelled her past a couple of empty stools at the counter and on toward a booth in the corner. Pride and pleasure made Marcy's eyes sparkle. Bruce Douglas was one of the most popular boys at high school. It was quite a feather in a girl's cap even to be with him. And to have him so obviously bent on keeping her to himself—Marcy smothered a blissful sigh.

Never, she was sure, had hamburgers tasted so delicious, or forty-five enchanted minutes passed so quickly. Bruce was easy to talk with, intelligent and amusing. He made a girl feel—Marcy groped for the key to his charm and likeability—as if she were important and that his main goal was to take care of her. No wonder every girl she knew was a little crazy about him, deep down inside, just hoping he'd notice her and get interested.

Well, Marcy thought, he's noticed me. And if he isn't interested, he's putting on a pretty good imitation of it.

She did her best to talk in a clever, spontaneous manner, to listen vivaciously, to fan his liking and keep it warm and alive. She didn't let the eager effort she was making show. But she was brighter, gayer, more witty than usual. The effort seemed easy with Bruce sitting there across the narrow table, smiling at her, laughing at the funny things she said, telling her about himself.

Marcy was appalled when she noticed how the time had flown. "I'll have to be getting home," she said. "This has been such fun, I didn't realize the time."

"Ten o'clock?" Bruce's brows lifted. "Why, the night's a pup. But I did promise to get you home early and I'm nothing if not a man of my word." He added, helping Marcy into her coat, "Besides, I don't want to get in bad with your parents. I might want to take you out on a real date sometime." Their eyes met and held for a minute and Bruce queried, "Would that be okay with you?"

"Of course," Marcy said, trying not to sound breathless.

It took only a few minutes to drive home. Bruce pulled up on the drive, then got out to walk Marcy up to the door.

"Thanks for the hamburger," she told him, "and the ride. Your car's just beautiful."

"I enjoyed myself, too," Bruce told her. "Lucky we happened to run into each other."

Something about the tongue-in-cheek way he said that made Marcy wonder if he had deliberately waited for her in the hospital corridor. Her breath caught with the delighted wonder of the thought. He did know she always visited Mr. Tuttle on Thursdays, but surely a boy as popular as Bruce Douglas wouldn't work out ruses just to run into Marcy Rhodes!

"Say," he said suddenly, "how about the senior play next week? Have you got a date for it?"

Never in her whole life had Marcy been so happy over the ability to say a simple, unequivocal, "No."

5

TO GO OR NOT TO GO STEADY

A ND to think," Liz said, as she and Marcy walked home from school together the next day, "it all came about because you did your good deed and visited an old man at the hospital! Maybe I should go in more for good deeds."

"The play's a week from tonight," Marcy said dreamily. "Bruce had plenty of time to ask anyone he wanted."

"Sure he did," Liz agreed. And she added, "I'll bet he was just sort of hoping he'd run into you at the hospital. He knows you go to see Mr. Tuttle on Thursday."

"Do you really suppose he remembered?" Marcy hoped he had, but it seemed almost too flattering to be true.

"I imagine so," Liz said. "Don't sell yourself short."

"I'm not," Marcy denied, switching her books from one arm to the other. "But after all, he can see me at school any time he likes. We're in a couple of classes together. Why would he bother to try to run into me at the hospital?"

"Maybe," Liz drawled, "he finds the smell of anesthetic romantic, or something. How would I know?"

Marcy laughed. "Men are sort of inexplicable sometimes, aren't they?"

"Practically always," Liz agreed. "When I was

47

younger, I used to think I had them all figured out. Now
I realize they're much more complex than the surface
indicates."

She sounded so glum that Marcy stared at her ques-
tioningly. "Are you saying that for any special reason?"

Liz nodded. "Hank Novak," she explained with a little sigh. And added feelingly, "The big lug!"

"Have you had a scrap?" Marcy asked.

"Not exactly," Liz said. "He's brooding, though. Has
been ever since the holidays."

"Because you went out with Bill?"

Liz nodded again. "The silly part is, though, I no
longer care a hoot about Bill Weaver. He's got so con-
ceited, he makes me ache. But I hated not to date him
a few times, with the old crowd home and all. I mean
Bill's one of the crowd; he's Steve's and Ken's age. Hank
wouldn't have fitted in nearly as well. And I went out
with Hank whenever he asked me. He and his folks
were out of town over New Year's, so I'd just have sat
home if it hadn't been for Bill. But when I try to get
all this across to Hank, he gives me that sad-eyed look of
his that makes me feel like a louse and says there's no
use discussing it, that he guesses we just look at things
differently. Honestly!"

"Gee," Marcy sympathized, "I didn't know you and
Hank were having problems."

"I thought," Liz went on, "if I sort of ignored the
whole thing, he'd get over it. Maybe it just takes more
time." She glanced inquiringly at Marcy. "How about
you and Rick? Didn't he resent your going out with
Steve so much?"

"I guess not," Marcy shook her head. "He just seemed grateful that I dated him some, too, even with Steve around."

Now that she stopped to think about it, Rick's attitude had been very broad-minded and mature. Of course, they were just good friends, but even so, he might have got mad over her spending so much time with Steve. Her heart warmed toward him, realizing his tolerance.

"You're lucky," Liz said. "Hank's so darned possessive, that's the trouble. He'd like to go steady, but I think that's dopey."

"So do I," Marcy agreed.

"Sometimes I'm tempted, though," Liz said, frowning. "I like Hank pretty well; I might even fall in love with him eventually—who knows? And going steady's one way to insure yourself a date for everything that comes along, especially the prom."

"But that's months off yet," Marcy objected.

"I know," her friend nodded, "but you've got to look ahead. It would be ghastly not to get invited and a lot of girls don't. I felt so sorry for some of the seniors last year, working their heads off on decorations and programs and all and then not being asked to go. It's rough!"

"Well, yes," Marcy admitted, "but you've always had dates for everything you wanted to go to at school. Why, you're so popular, I can't imagine you worrying over anything like that."

"I'm not exactly worried," Liz said slowly, "but you have to be realistic, Marce. Look how many seniors are going steady. The majority, wouldn't you say? You practically were last year, yourself, when Steve was around. And you were only a junior then."

"Well, Steve and I certainly never said we were going steady," Marcy argued. "If anyone else had asked me for a date, I'd have gone out with him. In fact, I did date a few other fellows."

"Darned few," Liz said. "The thing is, the way it is at Westfield High, if you go out with anyone a few times, people assume you're going steady whether you are or not. So that makes it practically amount to the same thing, because other fellows don't ask you for dates. It's getting," Liz finished regretfully, "harder and harder to play the field."

"But it's more fun," Marcy smiled at her.

"Yes, I know." Liz nodded. "It was funny, my mother and I got to talking about this same thing the other day. And she was telling me how different it was when she was young. Then, when a boy took you to a dance, you didn't dance the whole evening with him. It used to be that you'd just have the first and last dance with your own date—oh, and maybe one or two in between. All the rest of your dances would be with other boys."

Marcy's mother had told her about such things, too. It sounded rather strange, but exciting. It must have been fun to dance with a lot of different boys during an evening, no matter how well you liked the one you had come with. Marcy asked Liz, "And did she tell you about how they used to have a stag line, fellows who had come to the dance but hadn't brought a girl? They'd tap whoever you were dancing with on his shoulder and then they got to dance with you a while, until someone else tapped them."

"Yes, she did," Liz said. "And she told me how sometimes if a girl was real popular, she'd only dance a few steps with one partner and then be cut in on again."

"Or," Marcy amended, "if she wasn't very popular, her partner might be stuck with her and nobody'd cut in at all. That must have been awfully embarrassing for the girl."

"It sure would," Liz agreed. "But--it must have been quite a challenge."

Marcy nodded, smiling. "It would be living dangerously, all right. But I sort of like the idea, don't you? I wonder why they changed the system."

"Probably," Liz said drily, "the fellows didn't like it as well. But it must have been a wonderful whirl for the girls."

They had come, by this time, to Liz's house. "Come in a while?" Liz suggested.

But Marcy shook her head. "I've got too much homework and some housework, too. See you."

She walked the short way from Liz's house to her own, thinking about their conversation. Of course, it was Liz's affair, her decision to make as to whether she'd give in and go steady with Hank. But Marcy hoped she wouldn't. It wasn't that going steady was anything too serious. Lots of couples only went steady for a month or so and then made a switch. But it was the principle of the thing. When you thought the whole idea was silly, why should you have to conform, just because that was the accepted pattern at Westfield High? Why couldn't you be different if you wanted to?

That's what I'd do, Marcy thought, if I ever had to decide about it. Even if I *didn't* get to go to the prom!

But that prospect was so dismal she brushed it right out of her mind, as she turned up her front walk.

The ringing of the phone welcomed Marcy, that special rather long-drawn-out peal that seems to warn that it's been going on quite a while. Marcy dropped her books on the hall table and raced to answer it.

Her "Hello?" was anxious.

"Hi," Rick Whitney's deep voice said. "Where were you?"

"I just got in," Marcy said. "Liz and I were sort of dawdling along, I guess. We got to talking."

"Sorry I missed you after school," Rick told her. "I had to stop in the lab a minute and when I came out, you'd left. I was going to offer you a ride home."

"Oh," Marcy said, "I'm sorry, too."

They talked for a few minutes, so trivially that Marcy was beginning to wonder why Rick had called when he finally got to the point. "I was thinking about the play next Friday," he said. "How about me taking you?"

"Gee, I'm sorry," Marcy told him, "but I've already been asked, Rick. Thanks anyway."

"That's okay," Rick said. His voice sounded a shade deeper than usual. From disappointment? Marcy wondered. "Guess I should have asked sooner. Well—see you at school then."

"Sure, Rick," Marcy said. "See you."

Wasn't that always the way, she thought as she hung

up? Two dates for the same night, or none at all. She hated to have to turn Rick down. He was probably too shy to ask another girl. But the thought of going out with Bruce was really more exciting. Thinking of Bruce's good looks and popularity, the football letter he was entitled to wear on his sweater, his assurance and wit, Marcy felt her heart beat faster at the prospect of their date. And it would be a real date this time, one he'd asked for a week in advance, not just something that hinged on a chance encounter. She fell into such a pleasant daydream, the sound of the living-room clock striking four made her jump. She'd really have to get going if she wanted to finish her math assignment before time to start dinner. . . .

It was later that evening, when they were all sitting in the living room, that Mom passed along some news she'd heard at the hospital. "Mr. Tuttle is going home next week."

"Good," Dad said over the top of his paper. "Glad he's well enough."

Marcy looked up, frowning from her history book to demand, "Who's going to take care of him? Did he get someone?"

Mom nodded. "All of us have been keeping an eye out for a housekeeper for him. One of the nurses knew a widow right there in his neighborhood, a middle-aged woman with grown children, who wanted a part-time job. She'll come in at lunchtime every day and cook his meals and keep the house clean and leave when the dinner work's finished in the evening. That's all he'll need,

really. He'll be able to get around with a cane and he
can manage."

Marcy felt relieved. She'd been a bit worried over Mr.
Tuttle. Now that his leg was practically healed, he
couldn't stay on in the hospital. Nor would he want to.
Back in his own house, with a woman to take care of
him, he should be all right.

"Where does he live?" Dad asked.

"Over on Main Street," Mom answered, "in that block
of old houses just north of the gas station."

Marcy remembered Mr. Tuttle telling her that he
was born and raised in that house. After his parents
died, he lived there with his wife through her lifetime.
Now he was all alone.

Dad said, "That land around there is valuable, right
in the business section as it is. Probably one of these
days, when the few old-timers left there are gone, the
whole section will be razed and some modern stores
and offices will go in. Just a matter of time. He could
probably get a good price for his place now if he needed
the money."

Mom shook her head, smiling a little. "I'm sure he
doesn't want to sell. That's his home, where his roots
are. And he seems to have enough to last his lifetime."

Marcy was glad to hear that. She had never given any
thought to Mr. Tuttle's financial circumstances. But it
was good to know that he had enough to live in his own
house and pay his own expenses. After all, he was
seventy-four and, as he himself often said, "set in his
ways." And one of those ways, Marcy knew, was sturdy
independence.

In a way, the next week passed too quickly, in another it dragged. Marcy often found herself thinking ahead to her date with Bruce, dreaming the time away, deciding what she'd wear and how she'd talk. Then the minutes would slip past unnoticed. But if she got to wondering whether he'd really like her when they spent the whole evening together, what sort of an impression she'd make, even the seconds dragged endlessly.

When she went to see Mr. Tuttle for their last chess game before he left the hospital, he accused her, "Seems like you don't have your mind on the game tonight."

"I'm sorry," Marcy said. Then she confided, "I've got a very important date tomorrow night and I guess I can't quite stop thinking about it."

"Who with?" the old man asked interestedly. "Anybody I know?"

Marcy nodded. Bruce had looked in to say hello to Mr. Tuttle a few times, after she had told him about the old man. But Mr. Tuttle would never betray a confidence, so she went on to explain about Bruce having asked her to go to the play with him and how it had all happened.

"Hmmm," Mr. Tuttle said. "He's just a boy, ain't he? And you've been out with other boys before. What you worrying about?"

"I'm not worrying," Marcy denied. "It's just—well, he's so popular at school and this will be our first real date and—well, naturally, I hope he likes me."

"Be crazy if he didn't," Mr. Tuttle stated flatly. "Don't seem crazy, does he? Asked you to go out with him of his own free will, didn't he? Boys never used to do that in my day if they didn't like a girl and I haven't heard of any new laws being passed on the subject."

Marcy had to laugh. It was heartening to talk with Mr. Tuttle. He sounded so positive, she felt her own doubts and uncertainties drifting away, blown by the wind of his down-to-earth common sense.

She informed him, "You're very good for my morale, you know it? I feel much better. Of course, I'm going to make a good impression and naturally he'll ask me for another date."

"Sure!" Mr. Tuttle chuckled. Then, his attention returning to the chessboard, "Now that's all settled, go ahead, it's your move."

6

REAL DATE

THE night of the play was cold and clear and there were stars, but no moon as Marcy and Bruce came down the walk to his car. Marcy felt warm and happy, because Bruce had been so pleasant and completely at ease, meeting her parents and talking with them a few minutes with no indication of strain or boredom. She was sure he had made a good impression. Mom's eyes had flashed Marcy a message of approval and Dad had been cordial and talkative. It was so nice, Marcy thought, when someone you liked so well also seemed to be liked by your parents. She sighed a faint sigh of happiness and anticipation as Bruce helped her into the lush yellow convertible. She just knew it was going to be a wonderful evening.

When they reached the high school parking lot, it was already getting filled up, but Bruce angled the little car into one of the few remaining spaces expertly. "That's another good feature about these little jobs," he told her. "They park like a breeze."

"They ride wonderfully, too," Marcy said. "And there's so much more room in them than you'd imagine."

"She holds six real comfortably." Bruce grinned.

"More than that, we have to squeeze 'em in with a shoe-horn."

They had been talking steadily ever since they left Marcy's house, with none of those empty lulls in the conversation that sometimes developed when you were out with a boy you didn't know awfully well. Bruce was so easy to talk to, so responsive and amusing, she didn't feel as though she could ever run out of things to say. Sometimes when she was with Rick, they'd go for several minutes without a word. Only the funny thing was, with Rick that didn't seem to matter. He was so quiet, he made you feel sort of relaxed and quiet, too, but not uneasy about it, or awkward. Of course, with Steve, whom she had known so long and so well, conversation was never a problem. He was as easy to talk to as her brother. It struck Marcy, with a small sense of shock, how little she'd thought about Steve since he'd been gone. But then, he couldn't have been thinking about her too much, either. He hadn't even written.

The senior class had chosen *Our Town* for their play.

"Seems as though we might have picked something with a little more zip," Bruce complained, as he and Marcy got settled in their seats in the big noisy auditorium and began glancing through the program. "I like a musical better myself, or a good comedy."

"It's a wonderful play, though," Marcy objected. She had read it for extra English credit not long ago. And the simple reality of the story, the naturalness of the characters and the beauty of some of Thornton Wilder's lines had made an indelible impression on her. She added, "It's so real, like life itself."

"Pretty corny, though, in spots," Bruce said.

Marcy didn't agree, but she didn't want to argue, not with Bruce. She said, "It's easy to do settings for. And props were fairly simple. I'm glad they were, because I was on the prop committee and I have so little time. I don't know what I'd have done if we'd really had to scrounge around for stuff the way you sometimes do."

That reminded Bruce of last year, when he'd been on the prop committee for the junior play and an antique Victorian chair, borrowed from the science teacher's wife, had got broken. Marcy was laughing over his description of their efforts to repair it when she happened to glance about and saw Rick Whitney sitting a few rows ahead. She could glimpse only the back of his head and he didn't look her way. Marcy was just as glad. Rick wouldn't be too happy over seeing her with one of the most popular boys at school. He was sitting between Bob Finley and Harry Coates. As she had suspected, he hadn't tried to get another girl to come with him.

The lights dimmed then and the rustle of programs, the chatter of conversation that had lessened, but not ceased entirely during the overture by the school band, faded quickly. The magic of the play caught Marcy with the first spoken lines and she sat rapt and attentive, scarcely aware even of Bruce beside her, till he reached over and captured her hand. Her heart quickened, as her fingers curled in his. She had known it was going to be a wonderful evening.

During the intermissions they mingled with the throng in the corridor. The school seemed different at night, Marcy thought, with all the lights lit and a smattering of older people mixed in with the students and everyone all dressed up. The din was deafening and Marcy and Bruce contributed their share to it, talking and laughing and calling out to friends. They saw Liz and Hank some distance off and they waved, but couldn't push their way through to each other. Liz and Hank must have resolved their difficulties to some extent, Marcy decided, as they were both laughing and apparently having a fine time. Marcy hadn't had a private talk with Liz since the day last week when they'd walked home from school together. Her job on the paper meant that she usually had to go up to the journalism room for an hour or so after classes and Liz didn't like to wait that long. Marcy wondered fleetingly whether Liz and Hank were now going steady, or if Liz had won out.

When the play was over and the cast had taken their well-earned curtain calls, the audience began getting to its feet and heading toward the exits. Marcy looked around, trying to locate Liz and Hank in the crush. They'd probably walked to school, she knew, since Hank hardly ever had the use of his family's car. With two brothers older than he, one or the other of them always pre-empted it, according to Liz. Maybe, Marcy thought, Bruce wouldn't mind giving them a lift as far as Liz's house. But her seeking glance failed to locate her friend and so she said nothing of her idea to Bruce.

"I'm starved," he announced as they reached his car. "How about something to eat?"

"Sounds fine to me," Marcy agreed.

She had the Sweet Shop in mind, with the usual after-a-school-affair crowd filling the familiar booths and counter stools far beyond capacity. But Bruce passed the Sweet Shop without even slowing down and Marcy decided they must be heading for the Lighthouse. However, when they reached the highway, he turned the convertible in the opposite direction.

"Where are we going?" Marcy interrupted their animated conversation to ask.

"Relax, girl, and let me surprise you." Bruce grinned at her. "You'll like where I'm taking you. It's not far."

"Okay." Marcy smiled.

She leaned back, relaxed and happy, not counting the miles. After a while they turned into a sweeping graveled drive that led to a neon-lighted restaurant. TONY'S PIZZA was spelled out against the night sky in vivid crimson.

"Pizza," Marcy said. "Do you like it?"

"Don't you?" Bruce asked anxiously. "I'm crazy about the stuff."

"I don't know," Marcy admitted. "I've never had any."

"Then you haven't lived," Bruce assured her. "Come on."

TONY'S was bright and cheerful and there was a warm savory spiciness in the air that Bruce sniffed with enthusiasm. "Boy," he said, "smell that aroma! Tony's wife, Angelina, is the best pizza cook for miles around. You'll see."

Everyone seemed to be eating wedges of what looked to Marcy like big, golden yellow pancakes, with catchup or something tomato-y on top. "Is that it?" she asked Bruce.

He nodded. "We'll just order a plain one this first time. You have to sort of work up to the really fancy concoctions. But I'll make a pizza fan of you yet."

The place was half-filled with diners, most of them a bit older than the high school crowd. Not that there was anything wrong about that, but Marcy sort of missed the easy familiarity of the Sweet Shop. And she had a hunch she wasn't going to like pizza nearly as well as she did chocolate malts.

But, surprisingly, the hot cheesy-tomato-y dish that was soon served to them turned out to be quite tasty. Marcy nibbled at the first wedge a shade dubiously. Then she exclaimed, "Why, it is good!"

Bruce laughed at her indulgently. "Of course, it's good. Didn't I tell you?"

While they were eating, someone began to play an accordion and Marcy glanced around in surprise. The player was a dark, curly-haired young man, who seemed able to coax music of a singularly haunting variety from his instrument. He played music she had never heard before, Italian folk songs, Bruce said they were. Listening, Marcy could almost see peasant dancers in colorful costumes, whirling and dipping to the lively strains. The young man stood slouched and easy, his black eyes fixed far away, and wove a sort of magic that held the diners quiet. When he had played half a dozen numbers, he drifted off, ignoring the applause and Marcy turned to Bruce to say, "He's wonderful, isn't he?"

Bruce nodded. "Sometimes he sings, but only if he happens to feel like it. He's a character. No encores, no matter how many people are here, or how much they applaud. He plays as long as he wants to and stops. Anyway, he's better than a juke box. Want another pizza?"

Marcy shook her head. "It's too rich to eat a lot of. But I liked it."

"Good," Bruce said. "A girl after my own heart."

He paid their check and helped Marcy on with her coat. They went out into the chill night. The moon was up now and everything stood out in its glow, clear and eerily pale, almost like dim daylight. They got into Bruce's car and turned onto the broad four-lane highway. Heading back toward town, the convertible's wheels almost seemed to skim the road without touching it.

"Wish I could really let her out," Bruce said wistfully.

"You're going fast enough," Marcy told him. "We don't want to get stopped for speeding."

"I know," Bruce said. "I got one ticket right after I got the car and my dad really laid the law down then. I've been a good boy ever since."

They were back in Westfield in no time, turning onto Marcy's street, onto the drive beside the house. The porch light shed its welcoming glow, but Bruce drove far enough along the drive to be beyond its reach. He stopped the car and leaned back.

"There you are." He grinned at Marcy, his glance half teasing. "Home all in one piece and even before midnight. What's your deadline?"

"Deadline?" Marcy repeated.

"What time do you have to get in?" he asked.

"Oh," Marcy said. "Well, actually my parents never exactly name a time. They figure they can trust my judgment."

"I see." Bruce chuckled. "It's sort of like the speed limit in Illinois, no fifty or sixty miles, as they set it in some states, just reasonable and proper."

"I guess it is a little like that," Marcy admitted, laughing.

"And what do you consider reasonable and proper, on a night like this, with a moon and all and no school the next day?"

His arm rested along the back of the seat behind her and she didn't feel at all inclined to pull away. Her heart quickened, thinking what fun it was to sit here with him, talking and kidding, getting better acquainted. The way he'd spoken of making a pizza fan of her, it sounded as though he meant to ask her out again. Marcy hoped so. She said, her tone as light and casual as his, "Oh, we can talk a little while, I guess. Not too much longer."

His hand was on her shoulder now and he pulled her closer. "Don't be so aloof, then. I can't even make you hear me if you stay away over there."

He leaned his head against hers and Marcy liked the almost imperceptible fresh smell of his shaving cream, the slight roughness of his coat against her cheek. In fact, she couldn't think of a single thing about him she didn't like. If only, she hoped, he felt the same way about her.

"Come here," Bruce said, his voice very low and coaxing. He put his hand under Marcy's chin to tip her face up to his. But she turned her head, so that his lips, cool and firm and exciting, touched her cheek. "What's the matter?" he asked, still in that low, hard-to-resist tone. "Don't you like me?"

"Of course," Marcy said. "I like you—but—"

"But what?" Bruce asked reasonably.

"But—I don't just kiss every boy I go out with," Marcy said firmly. She tried to lean away from him, but his hand held her shoulder. "And—" she swallowed unhappily, "this is only our first date."

"Sure it is," Bruce agreed mildly, "but we'll never get better acquainted any sooner. It doesn't take more than one date for me to decide whether I like a girl or not. And I like you, Marcy. So what's the harm in a kiss?"

Marcy shook her head. "I'm sorry, Bruce. I—think I'd better go in now."

This time he made no effort to stop her when she tried to pull away. He just sat there, his glance level and faintly amused on her face, making her feel rather absurd. "Okay," he said, not sounding angry, just surprised, "if that's the way you feel." And he added, "But don't you think you're being a little childish?"

"Maybe I am," Marcy said, and the anger rising within her made her voice a little sharp. "But I don't call it childish not to want to kiss a boy the very first time I go out with him."

Bruce didn't even answer, just sat there looking at her in that maddeningly quizzical way, as though he couldn't quite figure her out.

"Anyway," Marcy said, opening the car door, "thanks for the play and the pizza and all. It was—very nice."

"You're welcome," Bruce drawled. He grinned then,

but it was rather a wry grin without much real amusement in it.

"Good night," Marcy said.

She got out and hurried up the steps too quickly for him to accompany her. If he even bothered to try, she thought woefully. She shut the front door and stood leaning against it, hearing the gravel hiss under the little convertible's wheels as he backed down the drive.

Well, all right! she told herself, feeling the hot sting of tears back of her eyelids and blinking them away. So he won't ever ask me for another date! So who cares?

But just the same, it hurt quite a lot to be so disappointed in anyone as she was in Bruce Douglas.

7

SATURDAY MORNING

I'M NOT surprised," Liz said the next day, when Marcy went over to her house to tell her all about it. "You shouldn't be, either, really."

Marcy had raced through her Saturday morning chores, not wanting to confide in Liz by telephone, but bursting to tell someone of her disappointing experience. If Mom had been home, she'd have told her. But this was Mom's Saturday on duty at the hospital and besides, Marcy had a pretty good idea what she'd say. "You were perfectly right, dear," Mom would assure her. "If he's as nice a boy as he seems, he'll respect you for it." Marcy felt she was right, too. But she felt equally certain Bruce wouldn't ask her for another date. Still, it might take the sting out of things a little to hash them over with Liz.

So now they were sprawled across Liz's bed and they each had a half-empty Coke bottle on the floor beside them. And Liz had handed down her sage pronouncement.

"Well, I was," Marcy said flatly. She flopped over onto her stomach and leaned on her elbows to stare into Liz's face. "Why should he expect me to kiss him right off like that?"

Liz responded by asking another question. "Didn't you want to?"

"Well—" Marcy considered for a minute, then answered honestly, "well, yes, I sort of did. He's so darned attractive and so much fun—and I like him—liked him," she corrected, "quite a lot."

"Don't kid me," her friend said drily. "You still like him."

"Maybe I do," Marcy admitted glumly, turning over on her back again and staring up at the ceiling. "But I don't like the way he acted."

"Now let's be logical," Liz said. "You admit you felt like kissing him—only you wouldn't so soon. Well, he felt the same way and how would he know whether you'd do it or not unless he tried?"

Somehow, put like that, it didn't sound so bad, Marcy reflected. "But he didn't have to act so—so superior about it when I wouldn't," she argued. "As if he were grown up and I was a mere silly child."

"Maybe you just imagined that," Liz pointed out. "He might have been a little embarrassed when you turned him down and didn't quite know what to do about it. The more uncertain a guy is, the more superior and sure of himself he tries to act."

"He didn't seem uncertain, or embarrassed, either."

"After all," Liz went on, "a fellow as attractive as Bruce probably doesn't get turned down very often when he tries to kiss someone. My guess would be, he could usually get away with a good deal on a date, even a first one. The thing is, he's so cute and any girl he takes out feels flattered by his attention and not inclined to do anything to discourage future dates. Oh, I don't mean you weren't absolutely justified," she broke off to assure Marcy. "But it was probably a sort of new experience for him."

Marcy nodded. "It all sounds very logical, the way you've got it figured out. But I'm disappointed in him just the same." She sighed and took a deep refreshing drink of her Coke. "And I'll bet last night marks the end of a promising friendship."

"I wouldn't doubt it," Liz said sympathetically. And she added, "I'm sorry."

"So am I," Marcy admitted. After a few moment's silence, it struck her that maybe Liz would like to discuss her own problems, so she asked, "How are things with you and Hank?"

"Okay at the moment," Liz said.

"Are you going steady?" Marcy asked.

Liz shook her head. "No, I stood my ground on that. But I compromised to the extent of promising I'd tell him if I dated anyone else. Honestly, why do men want to fence you in so?"

"I don't know," Marcy's tone was a shade wistful. "Personally, I'm not having any trouble that way right now."

The phone rang distantly then and a moment later Mrs. Kendall called out, "It's for you, Liz."

"That'll be Hank," Liz said happily. She bounced off the bed and headed for the stairs. "Stick around, though."

But Marcy said, trailing along behind her, "I've got to be going anyway. See you."

Liz's mother had gone back to the kitchen, so Marcy let herself out into the bright cold day as Liz began talking with Hank. She walked the short distance to her house briskly, although she really didn't have anything special to hurry back for. Dad was out doing some week-end errands. Mildred, their cleaning woman, had left the house in good order only the day before. And Marcy had done the breakfast dishes and made the beds before she went over to Liz's. Of course, there was always homework to do and she had a couple of sweaters that needed washing. Still, the day stretched ahead rather emptily. And the evening, too, Marcy thought drearily.

There was some mail in the box beside the front door and she fished it out with only casual interest. Even the sight of Steve Judson's big black scrawl on one of the envelopes failed to cheer her much. But she took it into the living room and curled up on the couch to open it. After all, a letter was better than nothing.

Steve started out by apologizing for not writing sooner, but he'd been so busy he just hadn't had the chance. With mid-term finals looming ahead, everybody was studying like crazy. He went on to mention a few campus activities that Marcy had already heard about through Ken's letters home. He asked how high school was going and congratulated her on being made feature editor of the *Breeze*. Evidently Ken must have passed that news along to him, since Marcy hadn't written Steve yet. She'd seen no reason why she should be the first to write. He signed the rather short letter, "Love, Steve," as usual. But he didn't say anything at all about the fun they'd had together over the holidays. And he didn't mention missing her.

Maybe he doesn't, Marcy reflected, folding the single sheet of paper and putting it back into the envelope. After all, he was busy at college; he was among friends. There were plenty of attractive girls around handy if he wanted a date.

Somehow the realization of all this didn't hurt as much as Marcy felt it should. She frowned a little, trying to figure out the cause of her strange, almost callous detachment.

She still liked Steve, she was sure of it. Yet they weren't as close, as important to each other as they used to be. Marcy knew this was true, or she wouldn't have just read his letter with no more vital interest than she might have read one of Ken's.

Was she getting over Steve, Marcy asked herself?

But she pushed the thought from her, not wanting to pursue it to any logical conclusion, unwilling to make up her mind just now. She was already sufficiently stirred up over Bruce.

She jumped up and stuffed Steve's letter into her blouse pocket and went upstairs to her room. There she found three sweaters that needed washing. Marcy had just run water into the basin and dumped in some soap flakes when the phone rang. She grabbed up a towel and carried it along with her, drying her hands as she hurried downstairs once more.

In response to her inquiring, "Hello?" Rick Whitney's slow easy voice said, "Hi."

"Oh, hi, Rick." A rich sensation of pleasure welled

up in Marcy. Good old Rick. No problems, no uncertainties, no disappointments. Nothing to be decided where he was concerned. Just a good dependable friend she could count on and have fun with.

They talked casually for a few minutes and then Rick asked, "Are you doing anything this afternoon?"

"Nothing special," Marcy admitted.

"Or tonight?" Rick asked.

"No," Marcy was growing curious. "What did you have in mind?"

"Skating," Rick said. "The river's frozen good and solid out here. There were some kids skating on it this morning and I expect there'll be more later."

"I'd love to," Marcy agreed. "I'm sort of out of practice, though. There hasn't been much ice this winter."

"We'll hold each other up." Rick chuckled. He went on, "My mother'd like to have you stay for dinner with us. Then I figured we could drive back into town and see a movie."

"That would be fun," Marcy agreed. "I'm sure my folks won't care. Dad will be home around noon and I can ask him then, but I know it'll be all right."

"Good," Rick said happily. "I'll be by for you at two if that's okay."

"Sure," Marcy told him. "I'll be ready."

After she had hung up she went back upstairs humming. The talk with Rick and the prospect of his plans for the rest of the day had blown away her feeling of sadness, her sense of being at loose ends. It would be fun skating on the winding river that edged the Whitney farm, being with Rick in the chill bright sunshine that would turn the wintry countryside into a sparkling wonderland.

And the prospect of dinner with the Whitneys was pleasant, too. Marcy had met Rick's family on the several occasions when she had gone out to the farm with him to ride horseback. And she liked them all. They weren't really farmers; they just liked living in the country. Every day Mr. Whitney drove to and from Clay City, where his job was. And Rick's mother, a cheerful woman with lovely prematurely white hair, seemed quite content to spend most of her time taking care of the rambling old white clapboard house and attending to the needs of her husband and Rick and his younger sister, Beverly.

Marcy finished washing her sweaters and hung them on the shower rod and the edge of the bathtub to dry. She noted then that it was almost noon and went downstairs to put on a pot of coffee for her father and start assembling cold cuts and cheese from the refrigerator for sandwiches. She was setting plates on the kitchen table for the two of them when the phone rang.

Maybe, Marcy thought as she moved to answer it, her father was phoning to say he'd be late. Or it could be Liz.

But to her complete surprise, Bruce Douglas' voice reached her ears and Marcy's heart did a funny little flip-flop.

"Why—hello, Bruce," Marcy said, with hardly—she hoped—a quaver to give away her astonishment. But she pulled the phone cord out far enough so she could sit down on the bottom step of the stairs, because her knees felt so wobbly.

"Where were you this morning?" Bruce asked. "I tried to call earlier."

"I was over at Liz's a little while."

"I wondered," Bruce told her, "if you were home and just not answering the phone because you were sore at me. But I decided it couldn't be that, because how could you know I was the one who was calling."

"I'd have answered if I'd been here," Marcy said. And she added, "I'm not mad at you."

"If you were, I wouldn't blame you," Bruce spoke seriously. "But I'm glad you aren't. Honestly, Marcy, I don't know why I acted that way last night. It was just —well, your attitude was sort of unexpected and I guess it threw me off base a little."

So Liz had been right, Marcy thought. He wasn't accustomed to having girls say no when he wanted to kiss them. And when one did, he wasn't quite sure how to take it.

"It's all right," Marcy's voice was a little choky. "I guess we just—sort of look at things differently. But you didn't have to call up about it."

"I wanted to call up," Bruce said firmly. "I'd like to get things straightened out so you won't think—Look," he broke off to ask, "how about me coming over right now? We could ride around and talk things over and—"

"I'm sorry," Marcy told him, "but I'm going skating this afternoon."

"I can skate," Bruce said, laughter edging his assured voice. "Let me skate with you."

"I'm going with someone else," Marcy explained.

"Oh." After a stretching silence, he asked, "How about tonight? You doing anything then?"

Marcy's throat ached with regret, having to tell him, "I've got a date tonight."

Another moment's silence. Then Bruce asked, his tone more serious than it had been, "Will you tell me the truth about something? This isn't just a brush-off, is it?"

"No," Marcy told him, "it isn't. I really do have a date. I'm—sorry it worked out like this." If only, she thought, she'd been in when he phoned earlier! But she hadn't. And Rick had called. It was all settled.

"Good," Bruce said and Marcy's heart quickened at the relief in his voice. "So long as it's not a brush-off, I'll try again soon. We've got to get some things settled between us. Bye, now. Be seeing you."

"Yes—all right," Marcy murmured and hung up.

She sat for a moment in a sort of blissful stupor. Then the hissing of the percolator bubbling over caught her ear. But Marcy didn't care how big a mess she had to clean up. That conversation with Bruce had been worth it.

8

RICK'S BRIGHT IDEA

MARCY had expected Bruce Douglas to haunt her thoughts most of the afternoon. But to her surprise, the combination of Rick's good company, the beauty of the sunny day and the exhilaration of brisk physical exercise, banished him quite effectively from her mind. She and Rick didn't have the winding river to themselves. Far from it. There were a lot of other skaters, several of whom Marcy and Rick knew and some who were contemporaries of Rick's thirteen-year-old sister. Most of the high school crowd skated off upriver a little way in order to escape the screaming antics of the younger kids. And a couple of the boys had the happy thought of building a roaring fire on the bank, which made a nucleus of warmth and companionship to which everyone kept returning.

The woods all about were stark black and white, with snow like thick cake frosting edging the tops of the branches and covering the ground with a white carpet, uneffaced except by occasional rabbit tracks. Over to the east the gray smudge of smoke from the Whitneys' chimney drifted straight up into the clear blue sky, so still and windless was the day.

Rick was a good skater and Marcy, after her initial feeling of awkwardness, got back into the swing of it

76

quickly. They raced each other to the river's bend and Rick won by a big margin.

"No fair," Marcy accused, "you've been practicing."

"I've only been out a couple of times all winter." Rick grinned at her. "Now that I know you enjoy it, too, we'll have to skate more often."

They joined hands and swooped back to the bonfire together, their skates scarcely seeming to touch the ice, then stood warming their mittened hands and talking and laughing with the others. It was a lovely day, a day to remember, Marcy thought. And Rick had given this experience to her. A little flame of gratitude flared up in her. He was always thinking of things to do that he felt she'd enjoy, like their horseback rides in the fall. They really had a lot in common, when you thought about it. A love of nature and the out-of-doors, an interest in writing and in poetry. Rick was fun to be with; his quietness was restful and there was strength about him, not only physical strength, but of the spirit as well. He was the kind of friend you knew you could depend on. And he had never, Marcy thought, tried to kiss her. She found herself wondering, just a little, what it would be like to be kissed by Rick. And, to her surprise, her heart quickened a bit and she felt oddly breathless.

Don't be silly! she told herself sharply. Rick isn't thinking about kissing you. He's too shy.

But her thoughtful glance dwelt on his face nonetheless as they stood there, shoulder to sholuder, warming themselves at the big fire, joking with the others. He had a good face, not handsome, but with regular enough features. Marcy liked the look of his mouth, and the firm chin beneath it. And he had nice eyes, too, wide-spaced and direct, a curious greenish shade of hazel.

"Why," Rick asked, "are you staring at me? Is my face dirty?"

Marcy felt the color flooding her cheeks, but she hoped they were rosy enough from the cold that Rick wouldn't notice. If he knew what she was thinking about, she'd die with embarrassment. She reached out a mittened hand and brushed the bridge of his nose.

"Just a speck," she fibbed. "Probably a little soot from the fire."

Rick rubbed a hand across his nose, too. "Okay now?"

"Okay," Marcy nodded, smiling.

The sun was getting low and blue dusk was settling over the snowy world. People began taking off their skates and starting to go and Rick said he thought they'd better be getting home too, as his mother had planned an early dinner so they could make the first show.

They took off their skates and got into shoes and boots, standing first on one foot and then the other, leaning against a tree. Then they started off through the snow toward the Whitney house, their skates clinking companionably together as Rick carried them.

He said, "The play was good last night, wasn't it?"

"Oh, yes," Marcy agreed. "I loved it." She wondered if he had seen her with Bruce. It was the first time she had thought of Bruce for hours.

"It's a good play, I think," Rick went on. "Simple, but it has a lot to say and it says it without too much beating about the bush."

"It takes a good writer to make just ordinary everyday life so gripping," Marcy said.

Rick nodded. "I'd like to write a play someday. I've even got a couple of ideas for it."

"Tell me," Marcy said interestedly.

But he shook his head, grinning. "Not till I get some more of it figured out. Then maybe I'll ask your opinion. That is, if you'd honestly tell me what you think and not just say it was good for fear you might hurt my feelings."

"I wouldn't do that," Marcy denied. "I'd always tell you the truth, Rick."

"I'd always want you to," Rick said, his tone serious.

Marcy had brought along a dress to change into before dinner. She didn't want to eat and go to the movies in the blue jeans and plaid flannel shirt she'd worn for skating. Rick's sister took her upstairs and showed her where the bath was and told her to come into her room across the hall to change her clothes. After Marcy had washed up, she went into Beverly's bedroom and found the tall, rather angular dark-haired girl brushing her hair at a pink-skirted dressing-table.

"What a pretty room you have," Marcy said.

Beverly thanked her and started to get up self-consciously, but Marcy told her, "Don't rush. I won't need the mirror for a while."

"Sure you don't mind if I stay?" Beverly's tone was a mixture of doubt and hope. "Rick said I wasn't supposed to stick around and bother you."

"You won't bother me," Marcy told her. And she

added, wagging her head, "Brothers! They're all alike, I guess."

"You mean you've got one?" Beverly asked interestedly.

Marcy nodded. "He's a couple of years older than I am. His name's Ken."

"Rick's almost five years older than I," Beverly said in much the same tone she might have used if she were saying he was forty.

Marcy's little laugh was muffled by the dress she was pulling over her head. "My brother's away at college now. And—would you believe it?—you actually miss them when they're gone."

"Yeah?" Beverly's faint grin was doubtful, Marcy observed as her head emerged through the neck of her dress. She said then, magnanimously, "oh, I guess Rick isn't really so bad. Only thing he gets awfully mad about is when I look at some of the stuff he writes and puts away in his desk."

"Well," Marcy said reasonably, fastening her belt, "wouldn't you get mad if he read what you'd written and put away?"

"He can't." Beverly giggled. "I don't write anything."

"I like to write, too," Marcy told her. "And sometimes when you first write something, you don't feel quite satisfied with it, you want to put it away for a while and then come back to it later with a fresh point of view. I expect it's that way with Rick, too, and that's why he doesn't want you to read some of his stuff. He isn't satisfied with it yet himself."

Beverly looked thoughtful. "I suppose it could be like that with him—only he never told me so."

"Sometimes," Marcy confided, getting her lipstick from her purse, "brothers don't take the time to explain things to their sisters the way they should."

Dinner was a pleasant meal and Rick's parents friendly and hospitable. The big dining room with its built-in corner cupboards and white painted dado hummed with talk and laughter. And Marcy had never eaten more delicious beef stew and hot biscuits.

Over generous helpings of wonderful apple pie, the talk turned to high school and Mrs. Whitney said regretfully, "It seems such a shame you seniors aren't going to get to take the Washington trip this year."

Marcy nodded. "We haven't quite given up hope yet, although Mr. Stevens said the school would never sponsor another one after the way last year's class carried on."

"What did they do?" Beverly asked round-eyed with curiosity.

"Oh," Marcy said, recalling the things Ken had told her about it, "there were only a few kids involved in the trouble. And it wasn't so much while they were in Washington and New York, but on the train going and coming. It's a long trip and there was too much goofing off and some of the boys had brought along stuff to drink. The teachers who were in charge just couldn't cope with it and of course, the principal felt responsible. That's why he said no more trips, even if Westfield seniors have been taking them for ten years now."

Rick said, "That's always the way. A handful of punks can spoil things for everybody."

His father asked, "Can't this year's class persuade Mr. Stevens you'd act differently?"

"We're surely trying," Marcy said. "There'll be an editorial about it in the next issue of the *Breeze* and the whole staff's putting everything we've got into it. All of us want to go, of course. It would be such fun and educational, too, seeing the government buildings and Mount Vernon and the U. N. in New York."

Rick said thoughtfully, "Too bad it takes so long to go. That's when the kids get to acting up—Say!" he broke off to exclaim, his face lighting with a sudden idea. "I wonder why we couldn't fly? That would get us there in just a few hours."

Marcy stared at him. "That's right. I wonder if Mr. Stevens ever thought of that?"

Rick's father suggested, "Seems as though the school could charter a plane, or a couple of them. There are usually a hundred or so students who go, aren't there?"

"At least that many." Rick nodded. "And I'll bet it wouldn't even cost much more if we could charter planes."

"Rick," Marcy exclaimed, her eyes dancing, "I think that's a terrific idea! Can I put it in our editorial? It would be something more constructive than just promising Mr. Stevens we'd behave ourselves. Would you care?"

"Gee, no," Rick said. "I'm as anxious for the class to get to go East as you are. Go ahead and suggest we fly if you think Mr. Stevens might go for it."

"If he does," Marcy said enthusiastically, "the senior class ought to give you a medal."

"Just a small one," Rick said with a chuckle, "platinum, with my name set in diamonds, would do. But what if he doesn't go for it?"

"We'll never know till we try," Marcy answered. "But our editorial next week is certainly going to have a lot more point than it would have otherwise, thanks to you."

"I'll tell you what you can do to repay me," Rick said. "If our dear principal is persuaded and if we get to go to Washington and New York and if we have an evening free from more serious sight-seeing, will you go to the Radio City Music Hall with me? I've heard so much about that place, I'd like to see it."

Everyone laughed as they started to push back their chairs and get up from the table. And Marcy told Rick, "That's an awful lot of iffing—but it's a date!"

9

POWER OF THE PRESS

MARCY passed along Rick's suggestion to the rest of the *Breeze* staff the very next time they gathered in the journalism room. And she wasn't surprised to find their enthusiasm matching hers.

"Now why didn't some of us think of flying?" Howie Clement, the editor, demanded. "Here we've been racking our collective brains—and I use the term loosely—trying to hit on some gimmick to give this editorial more point. So who comes up with a veritable lulu? A rank outsider merely talking off the top of his mind during a date with Marcy!"

"Quit beefing and be glad she dates such genius types," suggested the associate editor, John Harvey.

"And let's get cooking on the editorial," Jen Edson, the news editor, said firmly. "It'll have to be a honey to win Mr. Stevens over when he's made up his mind we're not going."

"Flying may be too expensive," Miss McCollum warned.

"Say, I could check on that!" John exclaimed. "My uncle's a pilot for T.W.A. He could give me at least a tentative idea of the cost of chartering planes."

"Check up at once," Howie barked, leveling a finger

at John in the best City Desk tradition. "And look into time schedules, too. The more solid facts we can write into this piece, the more our dear principal's likely to be impressed. And we have to impress him plenty or this year's seniors haven't got the ghost of a chance of going to Washington."

When the Westfield *Breeze* came out a few days later, there on the front page was an editorial plaintively titled, PLEASE, MR. STEVENS. It was an excellent piece of writing, brief, lucid, meaty and to the point. All the staff was agreed upon that, since everyone of them had contributed ideas and suggestions to it. Miss McCollum had told them she was proud of them, that she considered the editorial the best that had ever appeared in the *Breeze*. But would Mr. Stevens be sufficiently moved by it to reverse his decision to discontinue the eastern trip? That was the question.

Little else was discussed in the high school corridors during those first few hours after the paper appeared. And not only by the seniors, either. For if the principal did give in and let this year's graduating class make the trip, the possibility of future jaunts loomed ahead for all the others. So everyone was vitally interested in the developments.

The first result was a request by Mr. Stevens for Howie Clement to come to his office after school. Was this good or bad? No one was sure, least of all Howie.

"Don't be a hero and take the whole rap if he chews you out too hard," instructed the associate editor. "Tell him the entire staff worked on that piece and it expresses all our sentiments."

"I could always invoke the Fifth Amendment," Howie cracked, "if things get too tough."

"And come straight upstairs and let us know what happened as soon as you can," Marcy told him.

"We'll have our fingernails chewed down to the first knuckle," Jen Edson added ruefully.

The next half hour was an endless anxious time around the journalism room. Nobody got any work done, although they went through the motions. Matters weren't helped any by the fact that Miss McCollum wasn't there. She had a cold and had been away from school all day.

"Not that there's anything she could do," Marcy sighed, nibbling the end of her pen.

"Except lend us moral support," John Harvey added. "And I could sure use a spot of that."

Tension built up unbearably as the minutes passed. Then there was a sound of echoing footsteps in the hall and Howie strode through the open doorway. Deliberately he turned and shut the door behind him and emitted a restrained, but nonetheless enthusiastic version of the rebel yell. He leaped into the air, flapping his arms as though he were flying, and announced, "We're in, kids! Our editorial did it! Washington, here we come!"

Everyone fell upon him with excited questions and happy cries. Paralyzing whacks of congratulation rained on his back and shoulders.

"Have a heart!" Howie begged, struggling clear and taking refuge behind Miss McCollum's desk. "I don't deserve the credit. We all did it, remember? Or rather," he corrected drily, "we all did it after Rick Whitney gave Marcy the idea."

He proceeded then to give them a full run-down on his talk with the principal and its gratifying outcome. Mr. Stevens, Howie said, had been impressed with the serious and responsible tone of the editorial. All the research John had done on costs and time schedules had paid off. The principal had felt the students were attacking the problem in a mature and constructive manner and that he could do no less than consider their suggestions with an open mind.

"He came right out and admitted," Howie informed his enthralled audience, "that he had hated to discontinue the regular senior trip. I think he's grateful to us for pointing out a way in which he could try it again, with the element of that long train ride removed. And I took it upon myself to assure him that this year's seniors would act their age instead of goofing off like a bunch of nitwits. And we will," Howie finished fervently, "if I have to slug a few guys myself to keep them from spoiling things for the big majority."

"Then it's actually all set?" John asked.

"Well," Howie admitted, "there are details to be worked out, of course. Planes to be chartered, hotel reservations to arrange for, all that stuff. But Mr. Stevens talked as though that was just routine. After all, he's been setting up these trips for years. Our big job was to persuade him to go again—and we've done that. The rest shouldn't be anything to worry over."

Later, driving home with Rick, Marcy told him all about it. She had been surprised to find him waiting for

her. After all, classes had been over for an hour or more.
But it was like him to wait, so that she wouldn't have to
walk half a dozen blocks through the February drizzle.
He was always thoughtful. Sometimes it seemed to
Marcy that she took his unobtrusive attentiveness and
consideration too much for granted. He never failed to
be there when she needed him. And Marcy felt a warm
glow of pleasure now in his company.

She finished her rehash of the scene in the journalism
room by telling Rick, "And to think, if it hadn't been
for your bright idea—"

With customary modesty, he wouldn't even listen. He
interrupted, "Gee, I'm glad it worked out that way. Did
Howie find out when we'll be going?"

Marcy shook her head. "Not exactly. Sometime in
March, though. Before cherry blossom time, because
we can get a better rate in hotels then. Mr. Stevens tries
to keep the cost as low as possible, so more kids can afford to go."

"Good idea," Rick said. "After all, we can see lots
of cherry blossoms around here. Remember," he added
with a grin, "we've got a date to go to the Music Hall."

"I'll remember," Marcy promised.

That evening, when she told her parents that the
seniors would be taking the Washington trip after all,
she added a trifle doubtfully, "I got so excited over Mr.
Stevens' changing his mind, I haven't even stopped to
think about whether it'll work out all right for me to go.
Will it leave you in too much of a hole, Mom, with all
the work and everything?"

Her mother's laugh was teasing. "Now don't go martyr on us, dear. Of course I can manage for a few days. And you know we wouldn't want you to miss the trip for anything."

"Ken got a great deal out of it," Marcy's father said. "Had a lot of fun, too." And Mom added, "It would have been a shame if the actions of a few irresponsible youngsters last year had spoiled things for all of you."

Marcy spent a good half of that evening at the phone, retelling the wonderful news to Liz and the rest of her friends who weren't on the staff of the paper. In between phone calls she tried to do her homework, but it wasn't easy to keep her mind on her books. The thought of the trip kept fizzing up in her thoughts like bubbly ginger ale, making it hard to concentrate. But finally she managed to get her assignments for the next day finished. Closing her sociology notebook with a decisive snap, Marcy said, "There, that's that!"

She was alone at the desk in her bedroom, so no one answered. But Marcy felt companionable, so she loped downstairs calling cheerfully, "Anyone for hot chocolate? I'll make it."

Her parents, who had been reading in the living room, seemed favorably inclined to her suggestion, so Marcy went into the kitchen and began assembling the ingredients. After a mintue or two her mother joined her.

"I forgot to tell you before," Mom said, "we were so involved in the Washington trip—Mr. Tuttle went home today."

"He did?" Marcy asked interestedly. "He said last Thursday he thought he'd be going some time this week."

"I think he'll be all right," Mom said. "He can get around fairly well now with his cane. And his house-keeper seems competent. The only thing is, with her just there part time, I'm afraid he may miss having the nurses and internes around to talk to. He got to be quite a pet at the hospital."

"I hope he won't be lonely," Marcy said. "He's such a dear."

"He gave me," Mom told her, "a rather wistful message for you. He said he'd keep the chessboard handy, in case you ever had any free time. But he knows you're awfully busy."

"Not too busy for a chess game once a week," Marcy said, her heart swelling with affection and pity. "He knows I'll keep on with that, doesn't he, even though he is at home?"

"I think he's afraid to count on it," Mom said gently.

"Well, I certainly intend to," Marcy told her. "I'll call him up tomorrow so he'll know."

There was warm pride in the blue glance Mom bent on her. But all she said was, "Do that, honey. He'll be glad to hear it."

Marcy was just dropping a marshmallow into each steaming cup of cocoa when the phone rang. "You get it," Mom said. "It's probably for you anyway. I'll take Dad's and my drink into the living room."

Marcy carried her cup of chocolate along with her, sipping its delicious sweetness as she went to answer the phone.

"Hi." Bruce Douglas' voice startled her so that she set her cup down hastily lest she drop it. He hadn't called since that afternoon she'd gone skating with Rick, almost ten days ago. "I was afraid you'd gone to bed," Bruce went on, "when the phone rang so long."

"No," Marcy told him. "I was just in the kitchen."

"Did you hear the news?" Bruce asked. "The Washington trip's on again."

Marcy couldn't help laughing.

"What's so funny?" his tone was a trifle aggrieved.

"Nothing," Marcy chuckled, "except that I've been calling people all evening telling them the big news. And now you're calling to tell me."

"Of course, you'd know!" Bruce exclaimed, obviously struck by sudden realization. "I forgot you're on the paper. John Harvey told me. Isn't it great, though?"

"Wonderful," Marcy agreed blissfully.

They discussed the trip for several minutes, while she wondered whether he had called solely to pass along the news or whether he had any more personal reason for getting in touch with her.

As though in answer to her unspoken question, Bruce said, "Seems as though we ought to celebrate Mr. Stevens' change of mind some way, doesn't it? Are you doing anything Saturday night?"

"Well—no," Marcy murmured, wondering what Bruce had in mind, feeling hesitant and eager at the same time.

"How about driving over to Clay City with me to a show? We could start early enough to stop along the way and have dinner."

"Why—that's awfully nice of you, Bruce." Marcy felt herself pulled two ways more strongly than ever now. She liked Bruce. She'd enjoy going out with him again if she could feel sure he wouldn't act the way he had before. But—

As though sensing her hesitancy and the reason for it, he suggested, "How about doubling with Liz and Hank? Seems a shame to drive all that way with the back seat empty."

Marcy felt a weight lift from her mind. A double date would be just perfect. And Bruce had thought of it himself. He must want to erase any bad impression his attitude on their other date had left with her. And, certainly, she'd be very happy to meet him halfway.

She was so happy, her voice sounded just a shade quivery as she told him, "That would be wonderful, Bruce. I'd love to!"

10

DOUBLE DATE

AS MARCY had hoped, Liz and Hank fell in at once with Bruce's suggestion of a double date for dinner and a show.

"We never get over to Clay City," Liz told Marcy wistfully. "This will be a real ball for us."

"What I wish I could figure out," Marcy mused, "is why Bruce asked me for another date at all."

"Don't be so modest," her friend admonished. "Do you want me to enumerate your charms one by one? Apparently the guy likes you. Quite a few people do, when you stop to realize. There's Steve and Rick—"

Marcy broke in, "Rick's just a real swell friend and Steve—" a faint frown deepened between her brows, "well, honestly, Liz," she admitted, "I don't quite know how Steve and I stand any more."

"What do you mean?" Liz asked, her attention suddenly arrested, her gaze direct and questioning. "You still write, don't you?"

"Not as often as we used to," Marcy admitted. "And —well, it's funny about our letters. I write about things that are happening here. And Steve tells me what he's doing at Carveth. But we don't seem to have anything personal to say to each other any more. Sometimes,"

Marcy admitted, her tone troubled, "it's hardly any different than when I write to Ken."

"Gee," Liz said sympathetically, "that's too bad. Do you think it's just because you've seen so little of each other? Or do you suppose he's falling for someone else?"

"It could be that," Marcy said. "But you know, Liz, the thing that gets me—" she hesitated a second before coming right out and admitting this, then plunged ahead, "I don't even seem to feel vitally concerned about it any more. Last fall I'd have simply died at the mere idea of Steve going for another girl. Now my outlook's sort of—detached."

"That's not so hard to figure," Liz told her. "He used to be your one and only, but now you've got several to divide your attention among. And they're right here and he's far away. That makes a big difference."

"I suppose so," Marcy said, "but it makes me feel so funny and—fickle, not to be sure whom I like best." She sighed. "Everything was so much simpler when there was only Steve."

"We're too young to make up our minds anyway," Liz said airily. "I hope to meet scads of new men before I actually pick one for the rest of my life. The thing is," she informed Marcy, "you and Steve are starting to get over each other and it's always hard for a girl to face the fact that what she thought was the great love of her life is just developing into a nice easy friendship."

"Don't talk as though we're all washed up," Marcy objected. "I still like him a lot—only I'm not sure I like him the best of all any more."

"He was your first boy friend," Liz pointed out. "That

always makes it tougher. But a girl would have to be out of her mind to pass up someone as terrific as Bruce for a guy she only gets to see when he's home from college. And speaking of Bruce, it seems to me we were talking about him in the first place. How did we get over onto Steve?"

Marcy shook her head. She wasn't quite sure why their conversation had taken the turn it had. Liz went on, "You're lucky to have Bruce interested in you, know that? Half the girls in the class are crazy about him. He can date anyone he wants; all he has to do is quirk one of those quizzical eyebrows."

"I know," Marcy's tone was troubled. "That's another thing that bothers me. I'm not quite sure if that isn't one of the reasons I find him so attractive, because I feel flattered at his noticing me at all."

"Who needs reasons?" Liz sighed wistfully. "Just count your blessings and don't think so much."

"But I like to think," Marcy insisted. "I like to try to figure things out and understand all the whys and wherefores."

Liz shook her head. "Not me. I prefer just to relax and enjoy myself and not get all tied up in knots as to why I like one fellow better than another."

Maybe, Marcy thought, Liz had the right idea. She wished she could take things in her stride as casually. . . .

Saturday night's double date was even more fun than Marcy had anticipated. The four of them proved to be quite congenial and they talked and laughed all the way to Clay City, while Bruce's little yellow convertible ate up the miles. On the outskirts of the town, he pulled up at a big modern restaurant, all glass and stone. Obviously he had been there before.

"You'll like this place," he told them. "The food's terrific."

When they were seated and a waitress had brought them menus, Liz said almost immediately, "I'll have a hamburger."

Marcy realized she was taking it easy for Hank's sake. He never had a lot of money to spend.

But Bruce exclaimed, appalled, "Hamburger! That's sacrilege! The steaks here are delicious."

"They are also," Hank said firmly, tapping the menu with his finger, "three bucks apiece. Let my girl alone, will you? She knows I've got a hamburger pocketbook."

Bruce looked a bit embarrassed. He evidently hadn't thought of the money angle at all. But he said coaxingly, "You'll have steak with me, won't you, Marcy?"

But Marcy said doubtfully, "I don't think so. Steaks are always so big I can't eat half of them. Honestly, I'd rather have a hamburger, too."

"Well, okay," Bruce sighed. "But I think you're making a mistake. Hamburgers for four," he told the waitress regretfully.

After an enjoyable dinner, they went on to a movie. There were several theaters to choose from in Clay City and one of them had a picture both Marcy and Liz were eager to see. In the darkened theater, Bruce's hand closed around Marcy's and she felt her heart beat faster at his touch. The picture had some very sad moments and both girls sniffled a little over it.

Bruce leaned across Marcy to ask Hank, "Are your feet getting wet? The tears are almost ankle deep."

"Men are so heartless," Liz accused. "No feelings."

"I save mine," Bruce told her. "Why waste them on a movie?" His clasp on Marcy's fingers tightened just a little.

The trip home was as pleasant as the one toward Clay City, except for one small detail. Marcy felt a shadowy dread whenever she thought of the period, looming so close ahead now, when they would drop Liz and Hank off at the Kendalls'. Would Bruce's attitude be the same then as it had been on their first date? And would he be hurt and resentful if she didn't kiss him good night? Marcy didn't think she was going to kiss him, but she wasn't quite sure. Her feelings were all mixed up. It had been such a nice evening and she was grateful to Bruce. But unless she really wanted to kiss him when the moment came, she wasn't going to, no matter how he reacted to her hesitancy. It wasn't, Marcy reminded herself, that a good night kiss was anything so terribly special. But unless both people involved felt like kissing, the gesture meant less than nothing. And she wasn't sure—yet—that she was going to feel like kissing Bruce. She'd just have to wait till the time came and see.

Marcy snapped out of her absorption with a slight start as they reached Liz's house. They talked a few minutes, then there was a chatter of thanks and good nights and see-you-soons and Liz and Hank were walking hand in hand up the Kendalls' drive. Bruce drove on. In a couple of minutes, Marcy realized, they'd be at her house. And here she was with her mind still not made up.

Bruce turned onto the Rhodes' drive and stopped. To Marcy's surprise, he left the motor running.

She said a trifle breathlessly, "It was a wonderful evening, Bruce. I loved the show and the dinner and everything. Thanks so much."

"It was fun, wasn't it?" Bruce agreed pleasantly.

His arm rested almost impersonally along the back of the seat, not touching her at all. They talked for a few minutes, about the show, about the Washington trip.

Then Marcy said, "I guess I'd better go in now. It's getting late. Thanks again."

"That's okay." Bruce grinned at her amiably. "But next time you've just got to try those steaks. They're out of this world."

He slid from beneath the wheel to open the car door politely for Marcy, then walked with her to her door, said good night and departed.

Well! she thought blankly. Well!

Next day as she and Liz walked home from church together, Marcy asked her friend what she made of this abrupt change in Bruce's manner.

Liz considered solemnly for a moment, then suggested, "Probably he was anxious to erase the bad impression he'd made on you before."

"Well, I guess he did that all right," Marcy admitted, frowning. "Only now he's got me completely baffled. Honestly," she sighed, "men are so confusing."

"But fun, aren't they?" Liz laughed.

And Marcy had to agree.

One day early the following week, when Rick was driving her home from school, Marcy asked, "Would you mind stopping for a little while at Mr. Tuttle's house? It's not really out of our way and I want to welcome him home."

"Sure," Rick agreed amiably. "You've told me so much about him, I'd kind of like to meet him myself."

"I think you'll enjoy him," Marcy smiled.

Mr. Tuttle was delighted to see Marcy and he made Rick very welcome, too. "Any friend of Marcy's is a friend of mine," he announced with his dry little chuckle.

He introduced them to his housekeeper, Mrs. Watson, a plump cheerful-looking woman, then led the way into a little Victorian parlor, the tap of his cane muffled by the faded, but still lovely Oriental rug. Mrs. Watson bustled off to the kitchen for ginger ale and cookies, then went about her work.

"Your house is darling," Marcy said, looking around at the old-fashioned but graceful furniture. There was a lovely cherry-wood breakfront, its glassed shelves filled with colorful bric-a-brac. Mr. Tuttle sat in a comfortable wing chair near the marble-manteled fireplace, in which a fire smouldered against the chill of the day. Marcy and Rick drank their drinks and ate butterscotch cookies sitting on the red velvet couch with its ornately carved arms and trim.

"I'm glad you like it," Mr. Tuttle said. "I guess it's kind of fussy by present-day standards, but I'm used to it and wouldn't want to change." He added, his glance going to the tall, narrow windows and his voice sounding gentle, "My wife made the draperies herself."

"They're beautiful," Marcy said, and it was true. The years had dulled their colors into a soft pleasant tint.

"That's her picture on the mantel," the old man said. Both Marcy and Rick got up and went to take a closer look at the slender, dark-eyed woman in the outmoded dress, in the silver frame. "Helen, her name was."

Marcy smiled at him across her shoulder. "She's sweet."

"Yes—well—" Mr. Tuttle's voice sort of ended in a sigh. Then he said more firmly, gesturing toward a marble-topped table, "There's the chessboard all set up. Whenever you have time for a game, I'm ready."

Marcy said gently, "I can't today. But how about tomorrow evening? I'll take you on then if you like."

"Chess," Rick said, "is a game I've always wanted to learn. It sounds interesting."

"Oh, it is." Mr. Tuttle wagged his head. "And you've just got yourself an instructor, my boy. In fact," he suggested, "why don't you come along with Marcy tomorrow night? Then you could watch and pick up some pointers, get the general idea."

"Swell," Rick said. "I'd like that."

Did Mr. Tuttle actually wink at Rick, Marcy wondered, or was it just an involuntary contraction of the eye? If Rick winked back, her glance at him wasn't quick enough to catch him. But he looked almost too innocent.

When they left a short while later, Marcy told Rick,

"You really don't have to come along tomorrow night unless you want to."

Rick's grin had a slightly mystifying air about it. "You just shush now," he answered. "Mr. Tuttle invited me and he and I understand each other perfectly."

11

SURPRISE VISIT

LATE in February Ken came home for a week end. He had warned no one of his intention; his visit was a complete surprise. He simply breezed in Saturday morning while Marcy and her parents were finishing a leisurely breakfast.

"Food!" Ken beamed. "I hoped I'd make it in time."

It took a second for them to recover from their astonishment; then everyone began babbling questions. "But how—" "But what—"

Mom, happily lost in Ken's big hug, finished the first intelligible query. "Ken, what happened? Is anything wrong?"

He shook his head, grinning. "Not a thing. I flew in to Clay City with a guy who's got the sweetest little two-seater Aeronca you ever saw. Hitched a ride home from there. Glad to see me?"

"Of course," they all said at once.

And Dad added, "If you'd just let us know you were coming, we'd have met you in Clay City."

"If the weather had turned soupy we wouldn't have come," Ken pointed out, "and you'd have been disappointed." He yawned a tremendous yawn. "Only bad part about it was getting up before daylight."

Mom bustled about happily, frying bacon and eggs.

And Marcy got out fruit juice and poured Ken some coffee.

"Such service." He gave her a brotherly slap on the hip. "How you doing, kid?"

"Just fine," Marcy told him. "So busy I'm going around in circles."

"Steve said to give you his best." Marcy couldn't quite fathom the look that went along with her brother's words. Was there a touch of pity in it, or was she imagining things?

Mom was telling Ken how pleased she was that he'd happened to hit a week end when she had both Saturday and Sunday free from the hospital. "We can have a real visit."

"Sure we can," Ken agreed. "I don't have to get back to the Clay City airfield till two o'clock tomorrow. That gives us lots of time."

And somewhere, during all those hours, Marcy thought, she was going to manage an opportunity for asking her brother a few pointed and private questions.

It didn't take long for the main reason for Ken's unexpected visit to come out into the open. "There's this fellow in my fraternity," he explained, "a real fine guy—you'd like him. And he's got an uncle who runs a big luxury hotel in Miami. Right on the beach, fancy swimming pool, the works. Of course, it's not nearly full in the spring, when it's out of season. So he told Joe—that's the guy I know—he could bring down some pals and stay there for practically nothing. Joe's got a car, so the five of us he asked to go along figured we could take turns driving. That way we wouldn't have to waste time and money stopping and we could make it in twenty-four hours each way and have four or five days down there really living it up. And with expenses split six ways, you can see how cheap it'd be for all of us."

"Well, yes, I suppose it would," Dad agreed.

And Mom said, "Of course, we'd be sorry not to have you home, but it sounds like a wonderful vacation."

Ken nodded and his tone grew a little apologetic, continuing, "There's just one hitch. My allowance won't stretch to cover it. But I figured if you could see your way clear to advancing me just a little—say fifty bucks? I could pay you back when school's out and I get a summer job."

Dad appeared to consider the matter seriously for a long moment, but Marcy detected a twinkle in his eye that prepared her for his final decision. "It sounds like a reasonable request, son," he said, nodding, "in view of the fact that you've done better than I anticipated at living within your allowance since you've been away." He glanced inquiringly at his wife, "Don't you think we could take care of this for him, Lila?"

"I think so," Mom said. "It seems too good an opportunity to miss."

Ken breathed a heartfelt sigh of relief. "Now that's settled," he said, "I can really enjoy the week end. How about another cup of coffee, Marce?"

As she got the percolator and poured some into his out-held cup, Marcy asked, "Is Steve going to Florida, too?"

"Why, yes," Ken said, "matter of fact, he is. Hasn't he written you about it yet?"

Marcy shook her head.

"Of course," Ken reminded, "the whole thing just come up this week. You'll probably be hearing from him about it any day now."

"Probably," Marcy agreed.

That meant she wouldn't see Steve at all during spring vacation, most likely not until summer. And summer was months away. A vague disappointment stirred in her. Still, she didn't feel nearly as strongly about it as she might have. Her sensation was more curiosity than pain. She just had to talk to Ken alone and find out a few things.

Her opportunity didn't come until late that afternoon. Ken had gone over to Bix Meyers' house and Mom and Dad had driven to the store to lay in the usual week-end supply of groceries. Marcy was baking some gingerbread for dinner when she heard the front door open and her brother's step in the hall.

"You back already?" she called. "I'm out here."

"Bix wasn't home," Ken told her, coming out and peering hopefully over her shoulder. "What's that going to be?"

Marcy told him and Ken murmured approvingly, "Good. Lemon sauce to pour over it?"

"That I'll make later," Marcy said, "if you're real good and stick around and talk to me while I work."

"Sure," Ken agreed, sitting down and tipping his chair back onto two legs to stare at his sister amusedly. "And what would you like to talk about—as if I didn't know?"

"Steve," Marcy said. And she added, "It isn't so much that I care what he's doing. But I'm curious."

"Doesn't he tell you in his letters what he's doing?"

"All the unimportant things," Marcy admitted.

"Maybe he isn't doing anything important."

"Okay," Marcy said, "I'll spell it out." Getting information from her brother was like digging pearls out of oysters. But by the time she had the gingerbread in the oven Marcy had learned that Steve was still dating Thea, that it was quite a Big Thing between them and that Ken would not be surprised one of these days to learn that Thea was wearing Steve's pin.

"I feel like a low-down stool pigeon telling you all this," he complained. "Why are women so nosy?"

"Don't you think I have a right to know?" Marcy demanded.

"I'm not quite sure," Ken said in his easy, offhand way. "Have you told him you're dating two guys fairly regularly and that you like them both pretty well?"

"No, I haven't, but—"

"Okay, then," Ken interrupted. "Let's not go accusing Steve of holding out on you. These things just happen, Marce. Thea's right there at college. And your new guys are here in high school with you. It adds up."

"I suppose it does," Marcy said. She was surprised at how little she cared, really. It was exactly what she'd expected to hear when she started working on Ken. Even the element of surprise was missing.

"Maybe," Ken told her, "it'll be different next year when you're at college, too. But this absence-makes-the-heart-grow-fonder stuff is strictly for the birds, if you ask me."

Marcy spoke thoughtfully. "I don't think it'll be different next year. I think Steve and I are pretty well over each other. And you know what? I really don't feel bad about it at all, Ken."

"You don't?" her brother sounded surprised.

Marcy shook her head. "Steve was my very first boy friend and we liked each other a lot. We had fun together and I think knowing each other was a good experience for both of us. I hope we'll always be friends but—it's different now."

Ken sat there, tipped back in his chair, his blue glance quizzical and a little proud. "Your attitude," he told her, "indicates plainly to me that a suspicion I've long felt about you is true. My little sister has grown up. I can quit worrying about how she's going to react to things."

"Thanks, kid." Marcy grinned at him. "Those are kind words, coming from you."

"So do I get lemon sauce on my gingerbread?" Ken asked.

"A double portion, if you like," Marcy told him.

When their parents came in a little later, they found the house fragrant with the aroma of baking gingerbread and Ken and Marcy sitting cozily at the breakfast nook table, deep in a cut-throat game of double solitaire.

"Who's winning?" Mom asked.

"I am, natch," Marcy said airily.

"Only because she's got longer fingernails," Ken objected. "I get stabbed every few minutes."

Just like old times, Marcy thought happily, she and

Ken arguing and insulting each other and having fun. The little core of emptiness deep down inside her that had been engendered by his news about Steve was already closing and healing over. Soon it would be hard to remember it had been there at all. . . .

The two days Ken was home passed all too quickly. Then life settled into its familiar routine once more for Marcy. School. And hard but pleasant work on the paper. Enough housework to keep things running smoothly at home. A fairly regular Friday or Saturday night date with Rick. An occasional, and therefore a more exciting one, with Bruce Douglas.

It was on one of these latter occasions that they got to talking about the Washington trip. It loomed excitingly only a few weeks ahead now and the one hundred and twenty seniors who were lucky enough to be going talked and thought about it almost constantly.

"Tell you what," Bruce said, as they sat in his car on the Rhodes' drive, his arm resting along the back of the seat behind Marcy, "Let's make a date right now for when we're in New York. We can go to a night club, one of the famous ones you always hear about, the Stork, or Twenty One."

"But wouldn't it be terribly expensive?" Marcy asked.

"I'll start saving my pennies," Bruce kidded.

Marcy told him, "If we have two nights in New York, I'd love to. But I've already promised to go to the Music Hall."

"You're too popular," Bruce told her. "Who's my rival, Rick Whitney?" He didn't wait for an answer.

"Anyway, it should work out okay, because I've got it on good authority that we're going to have three days in Washington and two in New York."

"Good." Marcy smiled at him. "It's a date then."

After a moment, Bruce said, "I take it you don't believe in going steady."

"That's right," Marcy said. "You don't either, do you?"

Bruce shook his head. "I can't see this pinning yourself down to one person."

Marcy laughed softly. "You sound like my brother. He always said it was lots more fun to play the field."

"I don't feel like a brother toward you," Bruce told her wryly and Marcy felt her heart quicken at his tone.

Without thinking, she leaned her head back against his arm. It felt good, being close to Bruce. She seemed to belong there. Outside the car, the moon silvered everything to an enchanted brightness. She could feel Bruce moving closer. His arm tightened about her shoulders and she knew he was going to kiss her. And she didn't care. She wanted to be kissed by Bruce. This was the time and the place. Neither of them spoke. Their lips met and clung for a moment and parted.

Marcy's heart was hammering. Bruce's kiss had stirred her—whether more, or less, than she had expected, she wasn't quite sure. It wasn't an awkward, clumsy kiss, of that she was certain. Bruce had kissed other girls before. But it wasn't her first kiss, either. Could he tell that, she wondered?

"Marcy," Bruce said against her hair, his voice low and husky, "you're sweet. That was worth waiting for."

Marcy sighed. "I think so, too," she admitted in a small voice.

12

THE TRIP

O N THE front page of the *Breeze* was a composite picture made up of Times Square at night, the Washington Monument, Brooklyn Bridge and the Capitol building. Superimposed across all these was a cartoon drawing of three goggle-eyed seniors craning their necks in a plane labeled "Washington or Bust."

Marcy had written the two-column piece beneath the picture, captioned, "Seniors Take Off Friday on Five Day Trip." Still, even she had a hard time believing the great day was almost at hand. Along with all the others who were going, she was jittery with excitement and anticipation.

Friday was a beautiful day, clear and balmy for March. Two chartered buses transported the travelers and their luggage, sternly restricted to one bag apiece, to Chicago, some thirty miles from Westfield. Some of the students who hadn't flown before were a little scared at the prospect, although the two big silver planes awaiting them at the bustling airport looked safe and substantial.

Marcy wasn't in the least uneasy. She had flown several times with Ken in a little rented two-seater. And, as Ken had written, "If you can take that, one of the big commercial jobs will seem smooth as velvet to you."

All the girls were dressed up for traveling. There wasn't a pair of flat heels or bobby sox in sight. Marcy wore her green tweed suit with her tan coat thrown over her shoulders. On her lapel was the little corsage of violets that had been Mr. Tuttle's unexpected gift the night before. Marcy and Rick had stopped in to see him and say good-bye before the trip. And the old man had produced the little cellophane box of flowers with such sly delight that Marcy had felt her throat tighten as she thanked him.

"You're welcome," Mr. Tuttle had told her. "Be sure to send me a postcard."

Marcy had said she would. And she and Rick had both promised to drop in and see him as soon as they got back and to give him a blow-by-blow account of everything that happened.

"Do that," the old man had said with a chuckle. "And if you get a chance while you're at the Capitol, tell those fellows to quit spending us taxpayer's money quite so freely."

Marcy had to smile, remembering, as she sniffed the fragrance of Mr. Tuttle's flowers in the morning sunshine.

Liz and Marcy sat side by side on the plane and took turns at the window seat. There wasn't much to see, since they flew high. But occasionally a little doll-size town would be visible. And highways lay like spilled silver ribbons and rivers meandered lazily along in great curves. More often billowy white clouds blotted out everything and it was as if the plane flew over a vast expanse of whipped cream, with the incredibly blue dome of the sky far above.

The cabin was filled with chatter and laughter. Almost everyone enjoyed the trip, although a few felt squeamish enough to accept gratefully the seasick pills the stewardess offered them. Mr. Stevens had gone in the other plane, along with one of the teachers who were serving as chaperons. Miss McCollum, the journalism teacher and Mr. Hyde, who taught chemistry, were in charge here. But the students were on their good behavior, so that no display of authority was necessary. Marcy hoped, for the sake of future seniors, it would continue that way.

The trip seemed amazingly short. By lunchtime they had landed and were in their Washington hotel. But Mr. Stevens had told them not to take time to unpack now. Everyone was to report for lunch in the hotel restaurant in ten minutes. Sightseeing buses had been chartered to pick them up at one o'clock for an extensive tour of the city.

"Hardly gives us time to put on lipstick," Liz grumbled.

She and Marcy and two other girls were sharing a room, and it was filled to overflowing with their coats and luggage.

"Isn't it exciting, though?" Marcy exclaimed, as they all jostled each other at the mirror. "I just can't wait to see everything!"

They made a good start toward that objective the first afternoon. Observing Congress in session, visiting the Bureau of Printing and Engraving, having various other federal buildings pointed out to them by their rather harried guides, somehow seemed to make the processes of government much more real.

"It's one thing to read about it in a textbook," Marcy told Liz, "and something altogether different to be right here where it's all going on."

Liz nodded. "When I got my first real glimpse of the Capitol and the Lincoln Memorial—well, honestly, I got sort of choked up, didn't you?"

Marcy smiled at her. "I sure did. I don't even care how corny it sounds—I was thrilled!"

By the time they got back to the hotel at five-thirty, Marcy's feet hurt and she felt limp with exhaustion. But it was an exhilarated weariness that would soon pass. She and Liz and their roommates, Janie and Linda, flopped across the beds and started discussing who'd take the first shower.

"We can't waste much time lolling here," Janie pointed out, "if we're going to be ready for dinner by seven."

"And at a night club," Marcy yawned widely. "I didn't know Mr. Stevens had it in him."

"I'll take the last shower," Liz murmured, her voice muffled in a pillow. "I'm practically asleep right now."

"Okay," Janie said, jumping up. "Shall I go first?"

Everyone agreed, but Linda warned, "Nobody gets more than fifteen minutes in the bathroom, though."

As Janie reached across her for her suitcase, Marcy said, "This must be how sardines feel, packed in that little bitty can."

"Isn't it grand we're all so congenial?" Liz muttered, her eyes shut. "Leave some hot water for me."

At six forty-five when, by prearranged plan, all one hundred and twenty Westfield seniors assembled in the hotel lobby, everyone looked fresh and expectant. They walked the short distance to the Casino Royale and Marcy was glad when Rick and Hank joined Liz and her. There was so much to talk over, so many impressions to compare. The four of them sat together at the night club, enjoying the excellent dinner and amusing floor-show. Several tables away, Marcy saw Bruce Douglas with Sherry Clark, who was one of the prettiest and most popular girls in the class. It gave her a small qualm to see Bruce's fair head and Sherry's sleek dark one bent so chummily close together. Was Bruce feeling equally bothered to see her with Rick, Marcy wondered? Or had he even noticed?

When the orchestra began playing for dancing, a good many seniors took advantage of it. Liz and Hank were among the first on the dance floor.

"Sorry," Rick apologized, "I don't know how to dance."

"That's okay," Marcy smiled in spite of her disappointment. "My feet are about ready to drop off anyway."

"Yeah, sight-seeing's pretty strenuous."

He sounded relieved and Marcy thought it had been worth the small white lie to keep him from feeling inadequate. When she glimpsed Sherry and Bruce dancing smoothly past, she talked and laughed with Rick even more animatedly than before, just in case Bruce should happen to glance their way.

The next day flashed past in a bright montage of places seen and activities indulged in. The Washington Monument with its eight hundred ninety-eight steps, down which most of the class trudged lest they be considered "chicken" for riding the elevators both ways. The Congressional Library. The Unknown Soldier's Tomb, where Marcy was touched to tears by the inscription: "Here Rests in Honored Glory An American Soldier Known But to God." She was sniffling furiously when she felt a handerchief pressed into her hand and looked up to see Rick, not looking at her, but just standing there tall and understanding beside her. Marcy felt a warm little glow of liking and gratitude. Rick always seemed to be around when she needed him. Just how he managed it, she wasn't quite sure.

After lunch, they went by bus to Mount Vernon, with its gracious rooms and spacious grounds with the river flowing slowly past just as it had at the time of the Revolution. Marcy knew she'd never forget the rich sense of history, of timelessness, she experienced there. Even the souvenir shops outside the gates couldn't detract from that.

In the bus going back, she found herself sitting next to Bruce and she hoped it wasn't just accidental. "Didn't you love it there?" Marcy asked, still half lost in her dream of the past. "Wasn't it wonderful?"

Bruce nodded. "But I'm getting a little fed up with sight-seeing. Don't know whether I can absorb many more points of historical interest, or whether I'll start running over."

"You can relax tomorrow," Marcy laughed.

Their Sunday schedule called for church in the morning and then Mr. Stevens had said everyone could explore on his own, or rest, or do as he liked until two o'clock in the afternoon, when they would entrain for New York City.

"I intend to sleep all day," Bruce said feelingly. "And then, New York! That's for me." He asked then, "Is Monday night okay for our big date there?"

Marcy nodded. Rick had asked her to go to the Music Hall with him Sunday night. She couldn't quite resist telling Bruce, "It's okay if you're still sure you want to take me somewhere."

He frowned. "What brought that on?"

"Oh, nothing." Marcy shrugged, staring out the bus window. "I just thought you might have changed your mind."

"You wouldn't be jealous?" Bruce chuckled.

"Certainly not!" Marcy felt herself coloring.

"Well, good," Bruce said. "Because, for your information, I looked all over for you before I sat with Sherry last night. But you seemed all tied up with someone else."

Marcy turned from the window and smiled at him. The thought of Bruce looking for her *before* he sat with Sherry was most flattering. She felt proud and delighted.

"So don't forget our date," Bruce told her.

"I won't," Marcy answered. As if she could!

Sunday night it seemed that practically everyone in

the group had made dates to go to the Radio City Music Hall. Marcy and Rick doubled with Liz and Hank and they ran into a lot of others they knew in the big elaborate lobby. After a wonderful show, the four of them stopped at a nearby drugstore for sodas. But they all agreed they liked the Sweet Shop sodas better. "In fact," Liz said, "it makes me homesick to think of them!"

New York meant more sight-seeing. There was an extremely interesting tour of the United Nations buildings, a boat trip to Bedloe's Island and the impressive Statue of Liberty, another much longer trip by boat all the way round Manhattan Island. Not all their excursions were organized. Mr. Stevens allowed them some time to see things on their own. Some went to the Museum of Modern Art and some to Times Square; others shopped on Fifth Avenue, or took the subway downtown to see Wall Street and old Trinity Church. There was just too much to take in, even by cramming every minute to the fullest.

Marcy knew she would never, as long as she lived, forget her last night in New York. She was sorry to have to decline Rick's suggestion that they take a ferryboat ride over to Staten Island and back. But he was understanding about it and the vague unhappiness she felt was soon gone. Bruce and she double-dated with a friend of his, Ed McKay and his girl, Janie Coyle, who was one of Marcy's roommates at the hotel. And the evening was sheer enchantment from beginning to end. They went to the Stork Club, which was smaller than Marcy had imagined, but terrific just the same. The prices appalled her, but Ed and Bruce took them in stride.

"After all," Ed cracked, "this is a special occasion. So Janie gets nothing but movies and hamburgers the rest of the year."

"It's worth it," Janie sighed blissfully.

They ate and danced and kept looking around for celebrities. They didn't actually recognize any, but there were so many terribly glamorous people around, some of them must be famous, they felt sure. They stayed as long as they reasonably could and then Bruce had the bright idea of going up on top of the Empire State building and looking out over the city as a sort of farewell gesture. Naturally everyone agreed.

It was strange and rather mysterious away up there on the Observatory Roof, far above the street. The lights of the city spread below were like a fantastic garden, multicolored against the blackness. It sort of took your breath away with its magnitude. Marcy would have just liked to look and say nothing for a little while. But, of course, you didn't do that sort of thing on a date with Bruce. You were as witty and talkative as possible. And you laughed a lot. Even if you did feel somewhat awed, you covered up carefully.

Bruce and Ed were talking about a party that had taken place the night before in one of the boys' rooms. There had been a poker game and some drinking, quite a lot of drinking apparently. They had shoved some of the boys under the shower, to sober them up before they got too noisy. And they had amused themselves for a while, dropping paper bags filled with water down onto the street far below. One of them had just missed a policeman. Both Ed and Bruce thought this was terrifically funny.

Listening, Marcy hoped Mr. Stevens didn't find out. Only today at lunch, he had told the class how pleased he was with their behavior on the trip, how proud he was of them.

In spite of the bright lights all about, there were little pockets of darkness here and there. Janie and Ed found one of them and started kissing. And Bruce caught Marcy's hand and pulled her around a corner, where it was shadowy and they were all alone. His lips were cool and firm on hers and Marcy's heart quickened. Still, she felt ill at ease standing there. Lots of other people were up there on the Roof; someone might come around the corner any time. She wasn't even quite sure she liked being kissed by Bruce, although it was very flattering to have him want to kiss her. Marcy's feelings were all mixed up, uncertain. What's wrong with me, she wondered?

Almost like an echo of her thought, Bruce asked, his voice low, coaxing, "What's the matter, Marcy? Nobody's watching."

He pulled her close and Marcy could feel the strength of his arms, the scratch of his topcoat against her cheek. He had a right to expect a few kisses, really. He'd spent so much money on her, shown her such a wonderful time.

But she said, turning her face away, "I think we should go, Bruce. It's almost midnight and Mr. Stevens said everyone had to be back at the hotel by then."

Bruce stared at her for a moment and it was too dark for Marcy to be sure what his look indicated. He could be angry with her. Or he could think her silly. He might never ask her out again.

But whatever he was thinking, all he said was, "You're right. We are pretty close to the deadline." He put his arm through hers and they walked back around the corner of the building and Bruce said to Ed and Janie, "Hey, you two. Party's over. We have to be getting along."

"Already?" Janie said regretfully.

Probably, Marcy thought, that was the way Bruce wished she felt about it.

13

WISHFUL THINKING

FOR the first few days after their return, the trip filled everyone's thoughts and occupied most of the conversation. Then it began to assume the hazy outlines of a dream.

"Were we actually window-shopping on Fifth Avenue just a week ago?" Liz asked, as she and Marcy walked home from school Monday afternoon.

"Doesn't seem possible, does it?" Marcy agreed.

"Oh, well—" Liz shrugged philosophically. "I'm beginning to get down to earth. And in four more days comes spring vacation. I guess I can stand studying till then."

"And after vacation," Marcy reminded, "there'll be less than two months till we graduate!" That didn't seem possible either.

"I know," Liz replied. "If I had any head for math, I'd figure exactly how many school days that amounts to, even how many hours and minutes. But," she said meaningfully, "I do know one thing. The prom comes up the last Saturday in May. And it's none too soon to start laying the groundwork. Hank's already asked me and started saving his money. How about you?"

"Don't be silly." Marcy's heart grew heavy at the mere thought of the prom. "Who'd ask me?"

"That's a very defeatist attitude," Liz admonished severely. "You've got weeks yet. You should be able to work on someone."

Marcy sighed and ticked off the unlikely possibilities on her fingers. "One, Rick—he doesn't dance. Two, Bruce—he's ignored me ever since New York."

"Can't say I blame him," Liz frowned, "giving him the cold shoulder after he took you to the Stork Club."

"I didn't," Marcy denied. "I kissed him once. But I didn't want to stand there practically in public—" she broke off, then added frankly, "that's just an excuse, really. I didn't feel like kissing him any more. And if I didn't feel like it, it wouldn't mean anything. So why do it?"

"He's a mighty attractive hunk of man," Liz said. "Lots of girls would be delighted to kiss him." She asked then, her glance direct, "You're not still carrying a torch for Steve, are you?"

Marcy shook her head. "No, I'm all over Steve. And vice versa. We got everything straightened out in our letters. He's pinned to a girl at college and I don't care. We agreed that the way we used to feel about each other was fine while it lasted, that we wouldn't have missed out on it for anything. But now we're just good old friends."

"I guess you are over him," Liz agreed. "But then, why don't you fall for Bruce? Nature abhors a vacuum, they say."

Marcy laughed, admitting, "Honestly, I just don't know. Somehow my feelings about him get all scrambled."

"He could scramble my feelings any time he liked," Liz said soulfully. *"If* I didn't have Hank, that is."

"I've never been able to figure out why Bruce dated me at all," Marcy admitted. "You know I'm not a big wheel at school like Sherry and the other girls he goes around with."

"True," Liz said consideringly, "but it's obvious there's something about you that intrigues him. Maybe," she suggested, struck by a sudden idea, "it's because you *have* been sort of aloof with him. Did that ever occur to you?"

"No-o," Marcy said slowly. Then she smiled. "You mean—the thrill of pursuit and all that?"

"Sure," Liz pressed her point. "Lots of men—especially the popular ones who've been chased a good deal as Bruce has—are sort of taken with a girl who isn't too eager, one they really have to make a big play for before they get to first base. Could be that's your lure for him."

Marcy sounded dubious. "I doubt it—but it's an interesting idea. Anyway, we seem to be all washed up now."

"Not necessarily," Liz objected. "He may just be giving you a dose of your own medicine, playing hard-to-get himself. Personally, I'd be a little nicer to him, with the prom coming up."

Maybe, Marcy thought, Liz had the right idea. The prospect of not going to the dance at all was dismal. The Senior Prom was something a girl looked forward to all during her high school years. The very words had a sort of magic about them, a hint of soft lights and glamorous decorations, of heavenly music and a new dress, chosen with special care for this ultimate occasion. And, of course, a wonderful escort, someone you liked a lot, someone whose company would make the whole affair quite perfect and unforgettable.

Steve had taken her to the prom last year. And it had been a terrific evening. But the dance should be even more fun when you yourself were a senior, when you'd had a part in all the preliminary plans, when it would be your last high school dance. Marcy was on the decorations committee and their first meeting was scheduled for next week. How could she bear it, she wondered, to work on the decorations and then not get to go to the dance? That happened sometimes, but what a bitter, heartbreaking thing it must be. Still, it would be foolish to let her hopes mount too high. Because in spite of Liz's counsel, it seemed extremely unlikely to Marcy that Bruce would ask her to the prom, no matter how nice she was to him from now on.

However, she reminded herself the next time she ran into him at school, it wouldn't hurt to try. And so she stopped to talk a little while there in the corridor, laughing and animated, letting him know subtly that she enjoyed being with him, but not making it so obvious that he'd suspect an ulterior motive. He walked along with her to her next class and, when they were separating, asked casually, "Can I drive you home after school?"

"Gee, I'm sorry!" There was real regret in Marcy's tone. "I have to stay tonight and work on the paper."

"Ah, skip it," Bruce coaxed. "They can get along without you this once."

But there was too much work to be done and too few

people to do it. Marcy would feel she was letting the others down. "I'd like to," she shook her head, "but I just can't."

"Oh, well," Bruce said, "some other time."

He walked off down the hall with his jaunty stride and unhappily Marcy watched him go. Wasn't that always the way!

It was nearing four-thirty when she left the journalism room and got her things from her locker, preparatory to going home. Outside a chill rain was falling and the wind was raw. Marcy pulled her coat collar higher. If these were the April showers that were supposed to bring May flowers, she thought, they didn't feel much like it.

"Hi, Marcy."

She stopped in surprise at the sound of Bruce's voice. Then her eyes lighted as she saw his yellow convertible parked at the curb, the door open, welcoming her. So he had hung around more than a hour, waiting. That was a good sign!

Hurrying across the sidewalk toward him, her smile warm and wide, Marcy suddenly noticed another car, parked across the street. Unmistakably, it was Rick's old green one and the window was rolled down, so that she could see him, sitting there patiently. He was too far away for her to read his expression, but she was sure he wasn't smiling. Oh, dear! she thought, stopping for a second, uncertain what to do. But she was spared a decision. Rick reached out and rolled up the window and the car sloshed off through the gray day.

Then Bruce's hand was on hers, pulling her in beside him. And Marcy settled down with a little sigh, mur-

muring, "This is awfully nice of you," and trying to shut the memory of Rick out of her mind.

"It's such a foul day," Bruce said with a grin, "I hated to think of you getting soaked. Besides, I got held up myself, helping old Hyde set up a chemistry experiment."

So he hadn't just been killing time waiting for her, Marcy reflected. She wondered if Rick had. But there was no point in getting all stirred up about it now. After all, she'd seen Bruce first. And he'd asked hours ago to take her home. Rick wouldn't blame her. He was always understanding. She wished her throat would quit aching, though. Then it wouldn't be so hard to laugh and talk and seem gay and interesting to Bruce.

She must have succeeded well enough, however. Because by the time they reached her house some forty-five minutes later, after an enjoyable stop at the Sweet Shop for hot chocolate, they seemed to be on as good terms as ever.

In parting, Bruce said, "I won't be around during spring vacation. Our whole family's taking off for Virginia Saturday and won't get back till the Monday school starts again. But after that, you and I will have to get together."

"I'd like to," Marcy told him.

Later, rehashing it all with Liz on the phone, Marcy said, "So I guess he really isn't mad at me, after all."

"Good!" Liz exclaimed. "Did he mention the prom?"

"No and neither did I," Marcy said. "I certainly wasn't going to start hinting! But if we have a date when he gets back, it just might lead to that."

"I'll keep my fingers crossed for you," Liz promised.

That night as Marcy was getting ready for bed, Mom came into her room and they got to talking, as they often did. Both of them enjoyed these confidential times and it was only natural for Marcy to tell her mother about coming out of school and finding both Bruce and Rick waiting for her.

"I felt funny," she admitted, "but Bruce had asked to drive me home earlier. Only I hope Rick wasn't hurt." She went on then, frowning a little, as she brushed her hair, "The thing is, he won't say a word about it and I'll never know how he really feels. Sometimes I get— sort of mad at him."

"Because he isn't more demanding?" Mom smiled.

"Well, yes, I guess that is it. I've never known anyone quite like him before. I'm really fond of him. We always have fun on our dates—only—well, it's so easy to just sort of take him for granted, because he's always around when I need him. But if I don't, then he fades out of the picture kind of unobtrusively—the way he did today."

Mom said thoughtfully, "Sometimes, if someone likes you a lot, he may put your happiness ahead of his own. He may figure he wants to give you a free hand, to let you date other boys if you want to, but to be there in the background, handy and dependable in case you want him."

"Handy and dependable," Marcy said wryly. "That's Rick to a T. But he's certainly not the aggressive, dominating type. We've been going out together since last fall and he hasn't even tried to kiss me."

"Maybe," Mom smiled, "he's biding his time, waiting till he's sure you want to kiss him."

Marcy's heart gave a queer little lurch. She had never thought much about being kissed by Rick. Somehow it just didn't seem in character. But now that the subject had come up, there was something rather intriguing about the idea, something a bit unsettling. "Oh, I don't think so," she said, her voice a shade breathless. "I doubt he's ever kissed a girl in his life."

"Probably not," Mom agreed.

"In fact, I know he hasn't," Marcy said more firmly, "because I'm the first girl he's ever really dated."

"Some boys just get interested in girls later than others," Mom nodded.

"And yet," Marcy went on, "in lots of ways he's more mature than you'd expect at his age. He's very responsible and—well, he does a lot of thinking on important subjects, stuff that most of the boys I know haven't the slightest interest in. The world situation and politics, things like that. I guess that's why he's so interesting to talk with."

"He's an intelligent boy," Mom agreed, "and nice, too. Dad and I both like him."

"Oh, so do I," Marcy said. "He's a wonderful friend."

Mom said good night a few minutes later and went off to bed. Marcy turned out her light and opened the window and slid in between the cool sheets. Subdued night noises drifted in, the creak of a tree branch in the wind, the swish of tires on damp pavement as a car drove past, nothing disturbing. And yet Marcy couldn't fall asleep. She lay there in the darkness, thinking about

Rick, remembering him waiting there in the rain for her and rolling up the window and driving off, not knowing she'd seen him. What was he thinking, feeling? Did he resent Bruce? Was he hurt, or angry, or didn't he care?

I wish he'd tell me, Marcy thought.

Quiet people were so hard to understand. They kept things shut up inside them, things you couldn't be sure were there unless you delved and explored beneath the surface. Was she wrong in thinking their friendship was a casual thing to Rick, unfair in assuming that because he demanded so little of her he didn't hope for more?

Somehow the thought made her feel curiously breathless and stirred, as she had when she thought of kissing him. And she felt her cheeks grow hot with color in the darkness.

Determinedly, Marcy tried to push the thought of Rick away. But he kept coming back, infinitely more persistent in spirit than he seemed in reality. And Marcy's last drowsy reflection about him was a sad little regret that he didn't dance. But he didn't, so Bruce was her only hope.

Even half asleep as she was, Marcy realized that that was a very strange way to think of anyone so attractive and sought after as Bruce Douglas.

14

PICNIC IN THE RAIN

SINCE his return home from the hospital, Marcy had continued to see her friend, Mr. Tuttle, as often as she could. Sometimes Rick went with her on these visits. He had proved an apt pupil and was now capable of playing a creditable game of chess with the old man. And the two of them were quite congenial, discussing economics and politics and a variety of such subjects with lively interest. They didn't always agree, but this only made for more animated discussion. And both of them loved a good argument.

One afternoon, though, Marcy happened to drop in alone. Mrs. Watson waved her toward the dining room, where Mr. Tuttle had brightly colored seed catalogues spread across the table. "He's been poring over those all day," the housekeeper remarked, "and the frost not even out of the ground yet."

"It will be soon." Mr. Tuttle grinned at Marcy. "Now's the time to plan your plantin'. Just look at this rose."

Marcy pulled up a chair and sat beside him, exclaiming admiringly over a bush that produced three different colors of blooms. "It just doesn't seem possible!"

" 'Tis, though," Mr. Tuttle wagged his white head. "And I aim to have me some of 'em." He told Marcy,

"I've got your friend Rick lined up to do my spadin' for me when the time comes. That's a right nice boy, Marcy. I hope you appreciate him."

"Oh, I do," Marcy said.

The bright old gaze bent on her was inquiring. "Sure you ain't givin' him a rough time? He seemed a mite low the other afternoon when he stopped by."

"When was that?" Marcy asked with sudden interest.

"Let's see—day before yesterday, when it was rainin' so. Maybe the weather got him down."

"Maybe," Marcy agreed. But that had been the day both Rick and Bruce had waited for her and she had gone with Bruce. She asked, hoping she sounded casual, "Why did you think it might be my fault. He didn't—say anything, did he?"

The lined old face crinkled with his grin. "If he did, I don't know as I'd tell you. Us men got to stand together."

On a sudden impulse Marcy found herself telling him what had happened, explaining why she had driven off with Bruce. "That may not have had a thing to do with it," she said. "If Rick had mentioned it to me, I'd have told him how it was. But he didn't say a word."

Mr. Tuttle spoke gently. "He didn't say a thing about it to me, either—or about you, Marcy. 'Course, there's some things I can see without havin' 'em put into words." In response to her questioning look, he went on, "He's pretty gone on you. I know that by the way his face kind of lights up when he looks at you, or even when your name's mentioned if you're not around."

"But he never *says* anything," Marcy's voice was low.

"If I go out with someone else, he acts as if it's perfectly all right and he's not in the least concerned."

"Some fellers," Mr. Tuttle said solemnly, "aren't as competitive as others. They can be crazy about a girl, but it's just not in their make-up to try to elbow other fellers aside. They'd feel, if the girl really cared for them, she'd know it herself. And they wouldn't want her till she did make up her mind she liked them best."

Marcy's heart was beating so quickly it made her voice come out in a funny little quaver. "And you think Rick's that sort of person?"

"Don't ask me." Mr. Tuttle wagged his head. "You know him better'n I do. I'm just saying how some fellers are. You got time for a game?"

"That's what I came for," Marcy told him.

Mr. Tuttle beat her unmercifully. "Don't seem to me you had your mind on your playin'," he said drily when they had finished. And then he added, his old voice gentle, "Don't worry. Things'll work out. They always do, one way or t'other."

After her talk with Mr. Tuttle, Rick seemed to haunt Marcy's thoughts more than ever. It was strange how you could go along for months, thinking you knew a person quite well, not troubling to look below the surface. And then, for no very definite reason, something could start you wondering about him and you couldn't seem to stop.

She and Rick had had only casual encounters at school since the evening Bruce had taken her home. Yet Rick hadn't seemed hurt or angry. And he had asked her to go to the movies with him Saturday night. When he suggested the date, his manner had been exactly the same as always. But why shouldn't it be, Marcy asked herself? Nothing was changed between them. They were just good friends as before. She couldn't understand why she'd suddenly got into such a state of mind about him. He seemed to have developed into an enigma, a mystery. Or had he, she wondered? It was annoying the way all her recent thinking about Rick seemed to end in a big question mark.

She dressed for their plain ordinary Saturday night date with as much care as though—as though they were going to the Stork Club, Marcy thought wryly. Her crisp white blouse with the dainty lace ruffles, the black velveteen jumper that made her waist look so small, the merest touch of perfume. Marcy even considered wearing her heels, but this was just too ridiculous for a movie date. She didn't know what was coming over her!

By the time she'd finished fussing over dressing, Rick was already there. He and her father were deep in a discussion of government spending in the living room and Mom was sitting on the couch, knitting and putting in an occasional comment. Marcy stood in the doorway a full minute before anyone noticed her.

"Oh, hi," Rick said then, with his slow smile. "Ready?"

Marcy nodded, feeling unreasonable resentment rise in her. Why didn't he say something about how she looked? Of course, he never did, but if he liked her well enough to take her out at all, it seemed he might have acted a tiny bit aware of her appearance. Instead, he just helped her on with her coat and they said good night to her parents and went out and got into his old car.

"Well," Rick said as they drove along, "no more school for a week."

"Happy thought, isn't it?" Marcy answered. But she didn't sound very enthusiastic. She was still feeling a little illogically annoyed with Rick.

"You know what I did this afternoon?" he asked.

"No, what?"

"Got me a job," he told her, "out at the country club. I'll work all next week, helping get the grounds into shape. After that, I'll work Saturdays and it may develop into a full time deal this summer."

"Gee, that's swell," Marcy said, her grumpiness dissipated by the enthusiasm in Rick's tone. Part-time and summer jobs weren't too easy to come by, she knew. And Rick had been trying to line something up for quite a while. She added, "It won't leave you much spare time, though, will it?"

"Not much." Rick grinned. "But think of the money."

When they were settled in their seats in the darkened theater, he reached out and his big hand closed gently around Marcy's. It wasn't the first time he'd held her hand at the movies. And it didn't mean a thing more than it ever had, Marcy reminded herself sternly. There was no earthly reason for her heart to quicken so, or for such a glow of delight to settle over her.

After the show, they had their customary sodas and then Rick took her home. They sat for a while in the car, talking. About the movie they'd just seen. About

Mr. Tuttle. About school. Nothing more personal. Disappointment ached in Marcy's throat.

"You feel okay?" Rick asked a shade anxiously.

"Of course," Marcy said. "Why?"

"You seem sort of quiet." When she didn't answer, he went on. "I was hoping we could get in some horseback riding during vacation. Maybe have a picnic or something."

"How can we," Marcy asked, "with your job starting?"

"There's tomorrow," Rick said hopefully. "Would you like to ride a while tomorrow afternoon? If the weather's nice, we could pack some sandwiches and eat out along the way—that is, if you'd like to."

"Sounds like fun." Marcy felt her spirits lift a little. "You're sure Beverly won't mind if I ride her horse?"

"Of course not," Rick assured her. "How about if I pick you up around two?"

"Okay," Marcy said. "I'll bring the sandwiches."

When she went into the house a few minutes later, she was feeling happily elated. If she couldn't get things on a little more personal basis between her and Rick during a whole spring afternoon of riding and picnicking in the woods, then she wasn't the girl she hoped she was. . . .

The weather was on her side, Marcy thought delightedly when she awoke the next morning. As she walked home from church with Liz, she told her of her plans for the afternoon.

"My, gosh!" Liz exclaimed, her brows lifting. "You sound as if an old horseback ride and picnic with Rick is one of life's most delightful prospects. What's this big thing you've got with *him* all of a sudden? I thought it was Bruce you were going to work on."

"I'm not working on anyone," Marcy objected, not liking the sound of it. "I hope I get asked to the prom, of course. Who doesn't? But I like Rick and I think it'll be fun this afternoon. Anything wrong with that?"

"Well, don't flip," Liz said mildly. "I just find you a little hard to figure lately."

"Sometimes," Marcy admitted with a faint smile, "I can hardly figure myself. So I don't blame you."

The day grew warmer and balmier as it progressed. But while Marcy and Rick were saddling the horses in the Whitney barnyard, the sun slipped surreptitiously behind a rather ominous-looking cloud bank.

Marcy glanced up anxiously. "Gee, I hope it's not going to rain."

"So do I." Rick frowned.

They started out, riding side by side down the winding country road. But before they had gone a mile, big warm drops began to splash down and a reverberating roll of thunder made the horse Marcy was riding start skittishly.

"We'll have to get back," Rick called, turning. "Bev's horse hates storms and it's no good riding in rain anyway."

Marcy nodded, turning, too. They covered the distance back to the Whitney farm at a fast pace and rode in under the barn's shelter as the rain began to come down in earnest. They dismounted and Marcy helped Rick unsaddle and get the nervous horses into their stalls. Then they stood together in the wide doorway, watching the downpour.

"Fine thing!" Rick said disgustedly. "You're not wet?"

"Not enough to hurt any." Marcy took off her damp scarf and shook her hair free. "But it doesn't look too good for a picnic."

Rick peered out glumly. "Looks like an all-day rain instead of a shower, too." He added then, his tone troubled, "I'd ask you to have supper in the house, Marcy, but there's nobody home. My folks went over to Clay City to visit my aunt."

Marcy touched the knapsack of sandwiches and fruit and cookies she'd brought along and which Rick was carrying. "Darn it, I'm just in the mood for a picnic. We could take the stuff back to my house—or, I know!" She exclaimed, struck by a sudden idea. "Let's go and picnic with Mr. Tuttle. His housekeeper doesn't come on Sunday and I'll bet he'd get a big bang out of it!"

"Say, that's a swell idea!" Rick agreed. "As soon as it lets up a little, we'll make a dash for the car."

They stood there, talking happily for almost half an hour before the rain began to lessen. Then they discovered to their dismay that a great puddle had formed in a slight depression before the barn door and they were trapped there.

"Now what?" Marcy asked. But she wasn't really too concerned. "I feel like Alice in Wonderland," she told Rick, "after she cried all those tears and then got small and nearly drowned in the pool she'd made."

"Only you were always small." Rick grinned down at

her. The way he said it, it sounded like a compliment.

"Not so very," Marcy denied, although she did have to look up quite a way into his face. "It's just that you're so tall."

"Wait a minute," Rick said. "I'm getting an idea." He went off toward the back of the big barn and returned a minute later with a pair of muddy rubber boots. "I knew these had to be around somewhere."

As Marcy watched, he took off his shoes and put on the boots, stuffing the bottoms of his blue jeans into them, so that he was protected halfway to his knees.

"Now, then," he said and before Marcy quite realized what he had in mind, he had handed her his shoes and lifted her up easily into his arms and was carrying her out of the barn and across the big puddle and down the muddy path toward his car.

"This is a *very* nice way to travel," Marcy said. She had to put one arm around his neck, there was just nothing else to do with it.

"I like it." Rick grinned at her.

"Am I too heavy?" Marcy asked, just for the sheer pleasure of hearing him deny it.

"Of course not," he said. "You don't seem to weigh hardly anything."

Marcy felt just a smidgen regretful when they reached the car. She rather had an idea Rick did, too. But both of them were in excellent spirits driving back to town. And when they rang Mr. Tuttle's doorbell and announced to him cheerfully, "We brought you a picnic!" the way his old eyes lit with surprised delight made them feel happier than ever.

15

SAD LOSS

AFTERWARD, looking back, Marcy always felt thankful that the weather and circumstance had conspired to send Rick and her to Mr. Tuttle's house that spring evening.

"By gee!" the old man exclaimed, welcoming them. "It's sure fine to see you two! Sunday seems kind of long, here by myself. And when it's dark and rainy it gets downright depressin'."

"Now, none of that kind of talk," Marcy admonished. "We came here for you to cheer us up. We were going horseback riding and taking a picnic supper along and look what happened."

"So," Rick picked it up, "we asked ourselves whose house we'd rather have our picnic at, so long as we couldn't eat outdoors. And here we are!"

"By gee!" Mr. Tuttle said again, beaming.

While Marcy called her parents so they wouldn't worry about where she might be, the rain started to beat more persistently on the roof. When she got back to the living room, Rick had brought up some logs from the basement and was laying a fire in the old-fashioned marble fireplace.

"Oh, good!" Marcy exclaimed happily. "We can toast marshmallows after all."

140

Her lighthearted remark seemed to set the tone for the whole evening. Everyone's mood was relaxed and easy; conversation was effortless and interesting, and there was much laughter. They played chess for a while and Mr. Tuttle and Rick talked about the gardening the old man meant to do a little later on. Marcy discovered an old-fashioned wind-up phonograph back in the corner and a stock of ancient records, which were fascinating to listen to. Schumann-Heink and Elsie Janis and Caruso.

"Some of those are probably quite valuable," Rick told Mr. Tuttle. "Lots of people collect old records and they're not easy to find any more."

"Had 'em for years," Mr. Tuttle said. "Don't suppose there's anything newer there than Al Jolson. Helen used to like to play records, but I've got out of the way of it."

As the rainy dusk darkened outside the windows, Marcy set a table before the fireplace for their supper. "Actually," she said, "we should sit on the floor."

"And we ought to have a few ants," Mr. Tuttle said with a chuckle, "and some sand in the pickles for atmosphere."

"Let's not go all out for realism." Rick laughed.

"How about making some hot chocolate to go with the sandwiches?" Mr. Tuttle suggested. "Seems I should contribute some small share of this party."

So they had hot chocolate with their sandwiches and cookies. And they toasted marshmallows above the smouldering fire and ate them, browned on the outside and deliciously sweet and soft in the middle. The evening slipped away too quickly. All of them agreed it was one of the nicest picnics they'd ever gone to.

When Marcy and Rick were leaving, Mr. Tuttle told them, his old voice warm and happy, "Thanks, kids."

"What for?" Marcy demurred. "We had a wonderful time."

Rick nodded and said, "We sure did."

They said good night and ran out through the rain to Rick's car. Their last glimpse of Mr. Tuttle showed him silhouetted against the light in the hall, waving at them as they drove off.

"I'm glad you thought of going there," Rick said, his voice gentle.

Marcy was glad, too. And it was nice to know Rick shared her feeling. Some boys might have been bored with the way the day had turned out.

They were rather quiet, driving the short distance to her house. Rick stopped the car on the drive. He leaned back and stretched his arm along the top of the seat and, without any thought at all, just because it seemed the natural thing to do, Marcy leaned her head back against it. Rick laid his cheek against her hair and moved it back and forth slowly, as though he liked the feel of it. As for Marcy, she couldn't remember ever having felt happier. Maybe words weren't so important after all. Maybe, as Mr. Tuttle had said once, there were some things you knew without having to be told. Marcy felt sure just then that Rick liked her a great deal. His cheek against her hair, his hand on her shoulder, said it so clearly words would have been an overstatement. Marcy sighed a small shaken sigh and just sat there, savoring the moment.

But after a little while Rick did speak. He said, his voice slightly husky, "Gee, it's been a wonderful day."

"I know," Marcy agreed softly.

And neither of them was aware of the inconsistency of their comment, since it had been a rainy, miserable day from early afternoon on.

In fact, it was still raining when Rick walked with Marcy to her door a few minutes later. Their hands were clasped together and as they stood for a moment Rick reached down and his lips brushed Marcy's lightly before he gulped, "Good night," and hurried back to his car.

It was a clumsy kiss, unpracticed, inexpert. Marcy felt sure she was the first girl Rick had ever kissed. There was absolutely no reason why she should feel so exalted, so shaken by the beating of her own heart, so richly content. But who needed reasons?

The magic held over well into the next day. Marcy dreamed away the morning, going about her routine housekeeping tasks automatically. When Liz phoned, shortly after noon, they had a long lazy talk about all these things good friends can always find to talk about when they haven't seen each other for twenty-four hours. Marcy told Liz of the thwarted horseback ride and how Rick had carried her across the puddle and how they had ended up picnicking so enjoyably with Mr. Tuttle. But she didn't mention the kiss.

Now why? Marcy wondered as she hung up. Usually she had no secrets from Liz. But somehow the memory of the hasty unsettling touch of Rick's lips was too new and wonderful to share with anyone yet. Not until she'd had time to think about it a while, to try to figure out its terriffic effect on her.

The phone so close beside her shrilled again and Marcy started a little, lifting the receiver. Was Liz calling back to tell her something she'd forgotten? It couldn't be Rick. He'd be busy at his new job. "Hello?" Marcy's tone was curious.

"Marcy," her mother's familiar voice sounded strange and moved, "such a dreadful thing's happened. Mrs. Watson just called the hospital. She didn't know who else to notify. It's Mr. Tuttle."

"He's sick?" Marcy asked anxiously. Foreboding like a dark cloud bore down on her.

There was a second of silence before Mom said, "He died last night in his sleep, dear. Mrs. Watson just found him a little while ago when she went to work. Such a sad thing."

"But—" Marcy couldn't grasp it all at once—"but, Mom—he can't—it just isn't possible! Why, Rick and I were right there with him yesterday. And he was fine. He couldn't—" her voice broke and tears started from beneath her eyelids.

"He was quite old, dear." Mom's voice was gentle, pitying. "His poor tired heart just stopped. It's better this way, really—no long illness, or suffering—but I know how terribly you must feel when you're so fond of him—" her voice died away. When she spoke again, she sounded more like her usual brisk, efficient self. "I'm going to get off early, Marcy. I'll be home as soon as I can. And we'll see if there's any way we can help, anything we can do."

"Yes," Marcy said dully, numbly. "Yes, Mom."

But there was little, really, that they could do, then, or during the days that followed. Mrs. Watson proved calm and competent. And Mr. Mayhew, a rather fussy little gray-haired lawyer, who was the executor of Mr. Tuttle's estate, took over all details of the funeral. Mr. Tuttle, it seemed, had had definite ideas on the subject of funerals and had left specific instructions. He wanted everything over with quickly and simply, with no flowers and no one permitted to see him when he was dead.

"He told me," Mr. Mayhew admitted rather apologetically, "that he didn't want people looking at him when he couldn't look back at them."

Marcy could just hear Mr. Tuttle saying that, so completely in character did it sound. And she was glad herself that he had felt that way. She would so much rather remember him alive, as she had last seen him, waving a jaunty good-bye to her and Rick from his doorway. She was so grateful, deep down inside, that they'd been there with him on his last day. She knew he hadn't felt lonely, or left out, that he must have gone to sleep with pleasant memories. This was what she tried to think of when the tears pressed too hard against her eyelids. But sometimes they spilled over, just the same.

Mr. Tuttle's funeral was small. Marcy and her parents were there and Rick's mother came with him, although she had not known Mr. Tuttle personally. There was his housekeeper and his lawyer and a few nurses and internes from the hospital, besides a sprinkling of elderly people Marcy didn't know.

This was the nearest contact she had ever had with

death and when it was all over she felt drained and empty. Maybe, she tried to tell herself, Mr. Tuttle hadn't minded going. Maybe he was with his wife and had found the old friends who had gone before him. The thought brought some comfort. And time would dull the sharp edge of her sorrow even more, she knew.

"But I'll never forget him," Marcy told Rick as they walked together back along the cemetery drive toward the cars. "It was a privilege to be his friend."

Rick nodded. "He was a great old guy."

Marcy looked up at him, her eyes misty. She thought that was as good an epitaph as any. . . .

Certainly Mr. Tuttle's death cast a pall over spring vacation. But the days passed quickly just the same. On Friday a puzzling thing happened. Mr. Mayhew, the lawyer, phoned and told Marcy he wanted her to come to his office the next morning.

"At ten-thirty," he added in his precise voice, "if that is convenient."

"Well, yes, of course I can come," Marcy said frowning. "But—what for?"

"That," the lawyer said, "I should prefer to tell you in person. And will you be so kind as to have one of your parents accompany you?"

When she relayed Mr. Mayhew's message to Mom and Dad, they were as baffled as she. Then her mother had a sudden idea. "You know," she said, "it's possible Mr. Tuttle left you some little gift or memento in his will."

"I'll bet that's it." Dad nodded.

And Marcy felt a little surge of excited surprise. What could it be, she wondered?

It was Mom's Saturday to work, so Dad went with Marcy the following morning to Mr. Mayhew's rather musty office over the bank. Sitting in the large, dim room with its encircling shelves of lawbooks, Marcy felt her curiosity mount.

Across the wide, old-fashioned desk, Mr. Mayhew's swivel-chair squeaked slightly as he leaned back to extract a legal-looking document from a drawer. "This," he announced portentously, "is the last will and testament of Calvin Tuttle."

Marcy hadn't known Mr. Tuttle's first name until she had read the obituary notice in the paper. Even now it sounded strange and unfamiliar to her. Or perhaps it was just the lawyer's way of saying it that made her feel so queer.

"Since I am entirely cognizant of the contents of this document," he continued in the same solemn way, "I can give them to you in brief, which may—" he smiled a rather wintry smile in Marcy's direction—"be somewhat easier for the young lady to understand than legal phraseology."

Dad opened his mouth as though to say something, but Mr. Mayhew lifted a thin veined hand to discourage interruption. His bespectacled glance held Marcy's as she followed his words with unwavering interest.

"The estate," the lawyer went on, "is not a large one, but—ah—substantial, nonetheless. It consists of some fifteen thousand dollars, soundly invested at as high an interest rate as is commensurate with safety, plus the purchase price of the property at One-thirty-one Main Street, the sale of which Mr. Tuttle already arranged. Then there are the furnishings thereof, plus some family jewelry of undetermined value. And all of this property, real and personal, of any description, has been left to Marcy Rhodes, whom, Mr. Tuttle himself informed me, he considered a dear friend and the person who had done more than any other to contribute to his happiness during the latter part of his long lifetime."

"You mean—" Marcy's hand was pressed hard against her throat and her voice sounded a little high with utter amazement, "Mr. Tuttle left all that—to me?"

"That, my dear, is exactly what I mean. And if I may say so," Mr. Mayhew gave Marcy his rather tight-lipped little smile, "you are quite a fortunate young lady to be inheriting such a nice substantial estate."

But it wasn't the estate Marcy was thinking of. It was the wholly incredible kindness and generosity of her good friend, Mr. Tuttle.

16

SOMETHING WONDERFUL

HOW does it feel," Liz asked dreamily as she and Marcy sat in the warm spring sunshine on the Rhodes' front steps for an after-school chat, "to be young and beautiful *and* rich?"

"Don't be silly," Marcy smiled.

But although she didn't really think she rated any of those adjectives except young, she felt wonderful just the same. To be young and alive on such a day in late April was enough to make anyone feel wonderful. The soft little breeze ruffled her hair and carried a faint delectable scent of growing things. Lilac buds and the pale yellow of forsythia showed in the hedge. And the grass all about had begun to lose its winter brown and take on tints of rich green. Marcy drew a deep breath, and closed her eyes for the sheer pleasure of feeling the sun warm on her eyelids.

"If I had all that money," Liz said, "I'd do something really stupendous with it."

"Such as?"

"Take a Caribbean cruise, buy a whole new wardrobe, get me one of those cute little French cars—"

"Sure," Marcy said soothingly, "sure, you would. That's the way I used to talk."

"You mean," Liz asked, "the weight of all that wealth has made you go conservative?"

"No," Marcy had to laugh, "it's not that. But you can't seem to grasp the plain and simple fact that I haven't got it yet. There's the matter of probate and inheritance taxes and all that stuff. It takes time for an estate to be settled. Lots of time! The due processes of law, and I quote Mr. Mayhew, are *not* to be hurried. So just simmer down, honey. Eventually, I may do something real exciting with some of the money, take a trip or—well, anything! But right now, I'm no better off than I ever was, except for that lovely old garnet jewelry that belonged to Mr. Tuttle's mother and then his wife."

Just speaking of it reminded Marcy of the day she'd first seen it. Mr. Mayhew had informed her of Mr. Tuttle's request that she look through his desk personally, destroying the old letters and clearing things out generally. Her mother had accompanied her to the Tuttle house. Lila Rhodes had arranged for a leave of absence from her job at the hospital at Mr. Mayhew's suggestion. He had asked her to take care of readying the old house for being torn down, which was what the new owner planned to do. It had been sold with the stipulation that Mr. Tuttle was to occupy the house until his death. Now there was just the matter of selling the furnishings, some of which had proved to be valuable antiques, and turning the house over to its new owner. Lila and Mrs. Watson, along with a cleaning woman, had been hard at work that Saturday morning, while Marcy, in the crowded little study off the living room, had been going through Mr. Tuttle's desk. Actually, there hadn't been

much in it. Some old letters, which Marcy disposed of
in accordance with Mr. Tuttle's expressed wishes, some
receipts and bank statements and canceled checks, which
she put aside for Mr. Mayhew to decide about. Then,
in the middle drawer, she had come upon an old-fashioned ornately gilded jewel box. There had been a rubber band around it and, beneath the band, a folded sheet
of paper with Marcy's name written on it.

Wonderingly, she had opened it and read the short
note written in Mr. Tuttle's rather shaky but neat script.
In it he had thanked her simply for the many kindnesses
she had done him, the pleasure she had brought into his
life. And he had asked her to keep the contents of the
box, which had such sentimental associations for him.
The brief note was signed, "Affectionately, Calvin Tuttle."

Marcy's fingers had fumbled as she opened the box.
And her vision had blurred a little as she stared down at
the lovely old jewels on their bed of yellowed satin.
There was a wide gold wedding band, a lovely garnet
pendant on a fragile golden chain and an intricately
wrought bracelet of the same glowing red stones. Marcy
had sat there, tears running down her cheeks, knowing
she would treasure the beautiful jewels always, along
with the memory of Mr. Tuttle.

Now she came back to the present with a slight start,
as Liz said, "Garnet jewelry isn't something you're going
to get too much use out of. It would look a little odd
with sweaters and skirts, I'm afraid."

"But with a white formal," Marcy said dreamily, "it
would be terrific."

"Ah, yes," Liz agreed. "Something rather stark and simple, to show it off, something strapless, with miles of swirly skirt—"

She broke off then and Marcy knew she was thinking what a knockout such an outfit would be for the prom. Marcy was thinking along the same lines. Not that thinking did much good. And the prom was less than a month off now!

"No soap yet?" Liz asked sympathetically.

Marcy shook her head. "I'm pretty resigned, really."

"But I don't think Bruce has asked anyone else," Liz said. "At least, I haven't heard about it. Probably," she added, "he's holding off till he's sure who has the best chance of being chosen prom queen."

"That," Marcy laughed, "let's me out for sure!"

"I think it'll be Sherry," Liz said. "Or possibly Bett Kinley."

They discussed prom queen possibilities for a while, and then they got onto the subject of what Liz and Hank planned to do after the prom.

"He's saving his money like crazy," Liz said, "so we can go over to the Starlight Room in Clay City. He's laid the law down to his brothers, too, so we can use the car and won't have to depend on anyone else taking us. And don't think I'm not helping him save. We think twice before we have a malted these days, but I don't mind. The prom will be worth it."

Marcy nodded, trying to brush aside her own feeling of being left out, and concentrate on her friend's exciting plans.

"Of course," Liz went on, "some of the kids are planning to stay out all night long, but my parents said flatly I couldn't. Some of them are going to the dance, then out for supper at a night club in Clay City or even Chicago, then home to change clothes and pick up their swim suits and head out to the sand dunes. They'll be driving around practically all night and staying out the whole next day without any sleep at all."

"Sounds crazy," Marcy said. "They'll be dead on their feet."

Liz nodded. "Of course, there are always some who go in for the all-night deal. They say it's a prom tradition—" she broke off, contrite, to say, "Gee, Marce, I didn't mean to go on and on about the prom like this when you—"

"That's okay." Marcy managed a smile. "I told you I was quite resigned to not going."

"But if Bruce should ask you—" Liz began. Then she said, her tone reproving, "I honestly still think he might if you played your cards right. You said yourself he'd asked you to go out twice since spring vacation and you turned him down both times."

"Well, I already had dates with Rick," Marcy said. "I told you that, too. And I certainly don't intend to break a date with one boy to go out with another."

"No, I suppose not," Liz sighed. "But couldn't you sort of keep a Friday or Saturday night clear and see if Bruce calls before you make definite plans with Rick?"

"No," Marcy said firmly, "I couldn't. And you know why? Because I don't want to. I happen," she smiled, "to be quite satisfied to date Rick. Does that answer your question?"

"There you go," Liz shook her head, "getting all starry-eyed again. Oh, Rick's all right, if you happen to like the strong silent type. But the fact remains he doesn't dance. And the prom is approaching fast and it'll be your last prom, remember. Seems a crying shame to miss out on it."

Marcy jumped up. "Save your tears. I'll survive." She told Liz then, "I have to go in now and get busy. We're having a test tomorrow in sociology."

In spite of her brave words, the thought of missing the prom wasn't easy to take. But Marcy tried to put it from her during the days that followed. Then, on a Sunday afternoon, when she was lazing in the living room with her parents, the doorbell rang and Marcy went to answer it. To her complete surprise Bruce Douglas was standing there on the porch, looking very handsome in a tweed sport coat and gray slacks, his blond head glinting in the sunshine.

"Hi!" He grinned. "Busy?"

"Why, no," Marcy told him. "Won't you come in?"

"I was wondering," Bruce said hopefully, "if we couldn't go for a ride. It's such a terrific day. And I thought—well, maybe you might enjoy it."

"I'd love to," Marcy said, feeling her spirits lift. It was a lovely day and the prospect of a ride with Bruce sounded like fun.

She took only long enough to get a jacket and tell her parents what she was going to do; then she and Bruce went down the walk to his car and climbed in.

"How," Marcy asked, breathing the fresh clear air as they drove along, feeling the breeze whip her hair about her face, "did you ever happen to have such a perfectly scrumptious idea as this?"

"Oh, I'm full of scrumptious ideas." Bruce laughed. "You just never give me much chance to develop them."

Riding along, they were very gay, talking and laughing a lot, as they always did. But Marcy felt sure Bruce had something on his mind and eventually it began to come out into the open. He told her, "What I really wanted was a chance to talk to you. And seems as though I practically had to kidnap you to get it."

"Is this a kidnaping?" Marcy inquired.

"Next thing to it," Bruce nodded. "I don't seem to have such good luck when I call up like a gentleman and ask you for a date several days ahead. You always turn me down lately."

"Oh, Bruce," Marcy objected. "Just twice."

"*Just* twice," Bruce repeated and from his tone Marcy could tell that to be turned down at all was a new and rather disturbing experience for the popular Bruce Douglas. He said, "I've always had the feeling that I got off on the wrong foot with you the very first date we had. And that you still hold it against me, too."

"No, I don't." Marcy shook her head.

"Then why won't you go out with me?" he demanded.

Her smile was teasing. "I'm out with you now."

"I mean a real date," he persisted.

"But I will," Marcy told him. "It just so happened that I already had dates the last two times you asked me."

"With Rick, I suppose?" he sounded almost jealous, but Marcy hardly thought this could be the case.

"Well, yes," she said. "He asked me first. You wouldn't like it, would you, if a girl made a date with you and then broke it because someone else asked her to go out the same night?"

Bruce grinned at her across his shoulder, then turned his attention back to the road, "Do you have to be so ethical?" Before she could answer, he said, "I'm only kidding. Of course, I wouldn't expect you to break a date on my account. But I was beginning to think you didn't like me at all. That's not the case, is it, Marcy?"

"Of course not," she told him.

"Good," he said. "I'm glad we got that settled. Now then, how about next Friday night?"

"I'm sorry," Marcy answered, "but Rick asked me—"

"How about Saturday?" Bruce broke in, his jaw determined.

"Saturday would be fine," Marcy said meekly.

"It would?" he sounded elated. "Well, swell. Saturday it is, then. We'll go to the show and have pizza out at Tony's. Okay?"

Marcy nodded. It was really pretty exciting to have Bruce acting so masterful, so bent on getting her to go out with him.

He said, his tone beguiling, "No girl ever got under my skin before the way you have."

Marcy smiled and didn't say anything, because she wasn't quite sure what to say. She had a strong hunch that the reason Bruce was so interested was because he had thought she didn't care much for him—and that was a new and baffling experience, one he had to remedy right away.

"Why are you smiling like Mona Lisa?" he demanded.

"She's supposed to be so irresistible," Marcy said.

"You're irresistible enough," Bruce told her. "Quit it." And then, right there as they sped down the highway, he started talking about the prom. "I suppose you've got a date for that already," he said sort of broodingly.

"Why—no," Marcy's breath caught. "I haven't."

"You have now," Bruce said, "if you'll go with me, that is. Will you, Marcy?"

She drew a deep breath, scarcely able to believe her ears. Who said minor miracles still couldn't happen? Who doubted Santa Claus or fairy godmothers? Certainly not she. Not after hearing Bruce invite her in plain and simple language to go to the prom with him.

It wasn't easy for her to contain her exuberance sufficiently to say, with an effect of calm she was far from feeling, "Why, yes, Bruce, I'd like to." But she managed it.

How was she ever, she wondered, going to wait until she got home to tell Liz?

17

THE THWARTED SURPRISE

FOR a week Marcy floated on a pink cloud. Being invited to the prom was the key that opened the door to a shining world of delighted anticipation. Now she was one of the lucky company of girls who were already sure of a date for the big night. Now she and Liz could talk freely about new dresses and matching slippers, about hairdos and corsages, all the exciting preliminary details from which Marcy had felt excluded before. Now, too she could enter with greater enthusiasm into the work of the decorations committee, knowing that she was going to be there to see the climax of all their plans and endeavors.

The committee had chosen a Cinderella theme for the dance. As usual, it was to be held at the country club, since the gym at school was considered totally inadequate for this most important social function of the year. The club ballroom would be transformed with white and silver into a suitably glamorous background for the big occasion. There would be pumpkin coaches drawn by caricatured mice and glittering royal coaches drawn by prancing white horses parading around the walls. A larger-than-life-size fairy godmother, complete with magic wand, would loom near the entrance. Cinderella and her prince would occupy a place of even greater prominence near the bandstand. The senior art class had been pressed into willing service to execute these projects. And there would be dance cards made in the shape of dainty silver slippers.

"It all seems rather fateful," Marcy confided to Liz with a wry smile, "because I certainly would have felt like Cinderella if I hadn't been invited."

"Good old Bruce," Liz teased, "coming to the rescue like that."

Marcy's date with Rick on Friday night proved enjoyable as usual. There was a new roller-skating rink a few miles out of town, much patronized by the high school crowd, and Rick asked if Marcy wouldn't like to go there instead of a movie. It sounded like fun to her, even though she was a bit out of practice on roller skates.

"I went there last week," Rick told her. "Took Bev and some of her friends who were dying to try the place out, but didn't have any way to get there. It was fun and I got into the swing of it pretty quickly. It comes back to you."

Marcy said, with a little smile, "I'll bet Bev appreciates you. Come to think of it, you must make a mighty nice brother."

"Quit it now," Rick admonished. "Flattery goes to my head, you know."

They ran into quite a few people they knew at the roller-skating rink. It was a big, brightly lighted place and the click of skates, the persuasive rhythm of the music, the faint undertone of talk and laughter, spun a web of good cheer about the crowd. Marcy clung rather tightly to Rick's hands just at first, but gradually her feeling of confidence grew and she felt happily at ease. Some of the couples were spectacularly skillful, but most of them seemed content to skate along as Marcy and Rick were doing, enjoying the music and the invigorating exercise.

"This is fun!" Marcy exclaimed, when their first number was over. "I'd forgotten how I used to enjoy roller skating when I was little."

"I told you it would come back to you," Rick reminded.

"You skate so well," Marcy said, "you give me self-confidence, too. You have a nice sense of rhythm, Rick. It probably would be quite easy for you to learn to dance."

He gave her rather an odd look, which Marcy couldn't fathom. "Think so?"

She nodded. Maybe, she thought, his look denoted resentment. Maybe he didn't like her bringing up the subject of dancing, when she knew he didn't dance, and the prom loomed so near. Or maybe he thought she might be hinting that he should try to learn, during the few weeks remaining, so that he could take her to the dance. It was rather a ticklish subject any way you looked at it, Marcy decided. Better just let it drop.

She was glad to hear the music starting up again, to put her hands in Rick's outstretched ones and skate out onto the smooth oval rink with the rest of the crowd. And after that number, Rick suggested they go downstairs to the snack bar for a soda. There they ran into Jen Edson and Howie Clement, who invited them to share their table. Talking and laughing with the others, Marcy hoped that Rick had forgotten her ill-advised remark about dancing. Luckily, the conversation turned toward the school paper and then the Washington trip and nothing at all was said about the prom.

But later, driving home, Rick himself brought up the subject, to Marcy's surprise.

"The prom's only three weeks off now," he said. "From tomorrow night, that is."

"Yes, I know," she nodded.

"Marcy," Rick's voice held a little undertone of excitement she didn't understand, but the cause of which became increasingly apparent to her as he continued, "I've got a kind of surprise for you. I've learned how to dance."

Marcy's heart did a sickening little swoop as the full import of his words struck her. Her voice came out in a hoarse sort of gasp, "Really, Rick?"

He nodded and she could see his smile broaden as she stared at his profile. "I got Bev to teach me," he admitted with a chuckle. "She takes lessons, you know, and she's a pretty good dancer. My taking her gang to the roller-rink was really the pay-off. I had to do something big for her after all the time she's spent on me. Of course, I'm no expert, but I can now get around a dance floor without stepping on my partner's feet—much, that is!"

With every word he spoke, Marcy's heart sank lower. When he stopped talking, she said automatically, "That's wonderful, Rick."

They had pulled up onto the Rhodes' drive by that

time and Rick reached out to turn off the ignition before he went on, "I guess you know why I did it, don't you?"

"I—guess I do," Marcy admitted, her voice low.

"Because I want to take you to the prom," he told her. "That's what I've been working toward for weeks. Bev says I'm okay now and she's pretty critical. So, will you, Marcy?"

She couldn't speak for a moment, couldn't force her voice past the big aching lump in her throat. And it was like Rick to know exactly why.

"It took me too long, huh?" he said drily.

"Oh, Rick," Marcy gulped, "I'm so sorry. But Bruce asked me last Sunday. Up until then—" she couldn't go on.

"That's okay," Rick said comfortingly. "I don't blame you, for gosh sakes. A girl would have to be nuts to turn down Bruce Douglas."

"But I didn't know you were learning to dance," Marcy said miserably. "I didn't have any idea! If I had—"

"It wouldn't really have mattered, would it," Rick said quietly, "so long as Bruce asked you first?"

"I—I suppose not," Marcy admitted, wanting to be honest, wanting to say so many things she couldn't find words for. "The thing is, I was dying to go to the prom. And I didn't think I was going to be asked. Then, when Bruce invited me—well, of course, I said yes, even though—" her voice dropped a note lower, "even though I don't like him better than you—or even as well—"

"That's good," Rick said. He reached out and his arm went around Marcy and she leaned her head against his shoulder. He went on, his voice quiet, "I guess you know how I feel about you, Marcy. I'm not much good with words when it comes to—things like that. But I hope you understand. The way it is—" he paused a moment, then went on doggedly, "I want you to be happy. I guess that's the most important thing in the world to me right now. I knew you wanted to go to the prom. That's why I learned how to dance. But—it's okay, as long as you get to go."

"Oh, Rick," Marcy gulped. "I—I feel like crying."

"Well, don't, for gosh sakes," Rick said almost desperately. "It's okay, I tell you. Don't cry, Marcy."

She drew a deep breath. "All right. I won't. But I think it's perfectly wonderful, you doing a thing like that for me. I guess it's just about the most wonderful, thoughtful thing anyone ever did for me. And I'll never forget it. We—we can go to a dance together some other time, can't we?"

"Sure, we can," Rick said, rubbing his cheek against her hair.

"It would be such a shame to waste it—" Marcy began, then broke off, struck by a sudden idea. "Rick, promise me something!" she exclaimed, a note of determination in her voice.

"What?" he asked.

"Promise me that you'll invite someone else to the prom," Marcy said seriously. Then, as he started to demur, "I mean it, Rick. It would be silly not to. Here you've learned how to dance—and there are ever so many girls who are just dying to be asked. And I'd be happier if you'd go, really, I would. Please, Rick?"

"Well—I'll think about it," he said.

"No," she argued, "I want you to. Do it for me, won't you? So I won't feel so awful about not going with you myself? Then I'll know you're not mad at me for going with Bruce."

"But I told you that was okay."

"I won't believe it, though, unless you ask someone else," Marcy insisted. "And don't go putting it off. Ask someone tomorrow."

They sat there, arguing and discussing the matter for half an hour before Rick finally gave in and agreed to ask another girl. "But I won't enjoy it," he said darkly.

"Sure, you will," Marcy told him.

She turned her face toward him and their lips met. Rick's kiss stirred Marcy deeply. No longer did he seem clumsy and unsure, as he had the first time they kissed. She was aware of the shaken beating of her heart as they left the car and walked hand in hand up the steps toward her front door. And she thought how strange it was that your feelings for someone could cross an invisible line between friendship and something much deeper and more exciting, without your realizing quite when or how it happened. If only, she thought, she hadn't already said she'd go to the prom with Bruce, everything would be quite perfect. . . .

When she told Liz all about it the next day, her friend exclaimed, shaking her head, "Feast or famine, isn't that always the way? Two invitations to the prom or none at all!"

"But think of his learning to dance, just for me,"

Marcy said gently. "That's what I appreciate. He's so thoughtful."

"Yes, he sure is," Liz agreed. "But I still think you'll have more fun going with Bruce. Rick can't be a very good dancer that quickly. And besides, Bruce—"

"How well a person dances isn't everything," Marcy interrupted. "You have no idea how terribly I felt, having to turn him down when he'd gone to all that trouble. But he was wonderful about it. He's the most unselfish person!"

"I'm beginning to think you like the guy," Liz said drily. "Although how anyone could actually prefer him to Bruce—" she broke off to exclaim, "That's right, you have a date with Bruce tonight, haven't you!"

Marcy nodded. "But I'm not going to kiss him good night," she said firmly. "I—just wouldn't feel right about it when I like Rick so well."

Liz grinned. "For a rather quiet type, you do get involved in the most intriguing situations," she observed. "I don't know whether I can stand the suspense, waiting to hear how all this turns out . . ."

Marcy couldn't deny that her date with Bruce was quite enjoyable. His easy charm and high spirits always made him fun to be with. They saw a good movie and afterward drove out to Tony's for pizza. It was while they were consuming this spicy dish that the subject of the prom came up.

"The decorations are going to be simply terrific," Marcy told Bruce and proceeded to fill in some details.

"Sounds good," he nodded, when she finished. "And the music should be real cool, too, from all I hear." He added, then, with a little regretful shake of his head, "Too bad nobody'll be around very long to enjoy it all."

Marcy's brows lifted. "What do you mean?"

He shrugged. "Well, you know how it is. You get there around nine-thirty or so and leave maybe an hour later."

"An *hour* later," Marcy repeated in astonishment.

"Sure," Bruce said. "Only a few squares stick around much more than an hour. Last year they said the place was a morgue from eleven o'clock on. It's after the prom that the real fun begins."

"I see," Marcy said thoughtfully.

"Wouldn't you like to know," Bruce asked, "what I've got in mind for us?"

"Of course," she nodded. And sat there, feeling the pizza hot on her tongue, looking at Bruce and waiting, with a curious little sense of foreboding, for him to speak.

"Well," he said expansively, "first I figured we'd drive in to Chicago to a night club—either the Empire Room, or the Chez Paree, whichever you'd prefer. We'll get another couple, of course, might as well fill the back seat. Then we'll head home and change our clothes, get into jeans and pick up our picnic stuff and head out to the sand dunes—" he broke off, something in Marcy's face arousing a sudden dark suspicion in his mind. "You're figuring on staying out all night, of course," he asked, "and the next day, too? Everybody does it, you know, after the prom."

18

DISAPPOINTMENT

THE rest of the evening Marcy and Bruce discussed nothing but the prom and the extensive plans with which he wanted to climax it. Of course, she had known that some of the class would be chasing around all night and the following day as well, but she'd thought it would be just the wildest crowd, a small irresponsible percentage. According to Bruce, everyone would be celebrating in this manner, except a few squares.

"But with no sleep at all?" Marcy objected. "It sounds crazy." She went on, "I was at the prom last year. And we all went home after we had supper at a night club and slept for six or seven hours. Then we met again and went on a picnic."

"Did you?" asked Bruce. "That's not the good old Westfield tradition."

"Maybe not," Marcy said, "but it makes more sense."

"Who wants to be sensible on prom night?" Bruce objected. "I tell you, practically everybody will be celebrating my way. We want to do things up big, make it something new and different, an occasion to remember all our lives. We're free after four years of high school and this will be our night to howl. Just going to the dance and eating supper afterwards isn't enough. We've

167

all done that plenty of times. Prom night has to be special."

He was very persuasive, but Marcy could see glaring flaws in his argument. They had left Tony's by that time and were on their way home. The world beyond the windows of the little car lay drenched in moonlight and the road stretched invitingly ahead of them.

Bruce said, "Let's go for a ride. It's early yet and we have to get this thing settled. I had no idea you had such quaint old-fashioned notions."

Marcy said, "For one thing, I know my parents won't let me do it. Even if I was sure I wanted to myself."

"You can get around them," Bruce insisted. "Of course, you should have started months ago. Some kids I know have been working on the old folks since the beginning of senior year, dripping insidiously, like water wearing away stone. But you'll have to plot your strategy differently, go into a whirlwind campaign. I'll help supply the ammunition. I've got some left over from bringing my parents around."

"You mean they're actually willing?" Marcy asked.

He nodded, grinning. "Not exactly enthusiastic, but persuaded. I pointed out that everybody's going and, of course, they didn't want their poor son to be left out of all the fun. That's a good argument for you to use, too. Parents are a pushover if you can just get them to thinking they're standing in the way of their kid's pleasure." He added, "And, of course, you can always cry. That's where girls have a real advantage."

Marcy frowned. "I don't think that would work on my parents. They want me to have fun, but they've never gone along with the idea that a thing's all right, just because some other kids are getting to do it."

"Rugged individualists, eh?" Bruce chuckled. He made it sound like an insult.

"I like individualists," Marcy said coolly. "People who simply conform in every way, go along with the crowd—make me sick."

"You're cute when you get mad," Bruce told her. "I think you're an individualist, too. Maybe I like individualists and never realized it. Maybe that's your attraction for me."

Marcy had to smile. His charm wasn't easy to resist. She asked, "Who were you figuring on going with on prom night?"

"You," the word was soft as a caress.

"I mean what other couple?"

"Oh. Well, tentatively I'd thought of Curt Carson and Maggie Blair."

The names weren't very reassuring. Marcy knew Maggie only very slightly and Curt not at all. But he had the reputation of being something of a wild man. Some of his scrapes at school had been rather spectacular and she'd heard he was one of the drinkers on the Washington trip.

As though sensing the cause of her hesitation, Bruce said, "You don't want to believe all the tales you hear about old Curt. He's a character, but you'll like him fine. With Maggie and him, we'll have a ball."

"Bruce," Marcy's tone was troubled, "I don't know. I'm going to have to think this over, talk to my parents."

She added, "And hadn't we better be heading home now? It's pretty late."

"Okay," Bruce agreed mildly. "Whatever you say."

Marcy was quiet as they drove home. But Bruce was his usual amusing self. It was hard to think things through with him right there beside her, making her laugh every few minutes at his funny remarks.

When they pulled up onto her drive, he asked, "You're not mad or anything, are you?"

"No, of course not," she said. "I've just been—sort of thinking."

"If it's Curt that's bothering you," Bruce told her, "we can double with someone else. But I think you'd like him."

"It's not just Curt," Marcy admitted. "It's the whole idea of staying out, driving around all night. I'm just— not sure, Bruce."

"Don't be such a little square," he said, his tone teasing. "That's what the prom means, isn't it? A big night, the biggest night of our lives so far. Let's live it up."

"I know," Marcy admitted dubiously, "but—"

He didn't let her finish. "You sleep on it," he told her. "I'll bet you'll like the idea fine when you get used to it. And with the right approach, I'm sure you can persuade your parents. Remind them they were young once. They won't want to be the cause of your missing out on all the fun."

He didn't try to kiss her good night, apparently sensing that she wasn't in the mood. So Marcy didn't have that problem to contend with. But she had so much on her mind, she found it difficult to go to sleep. Had her parents been home, she'd have talked it over with them there and then. But they were playing bridge at a neighbor's. And so the whole matter kept churning around in Marcy's mind till she fell asleep out of sheer exhaustion.

Sunday morning breakfast was always a late and leisurely meal at the Rhodes' house, culminating just in time for them to get to the eleven o'clock church service. Today, with spring sunshine spilling across the table and sparkling on the silverwear, a rather glum Marcy proceeded to unburden herself of the problem that had haunted her dreams.

"I am supposed," she informed her parents without preamble, "to try to persuade you that it'll be okay for me to stay out all night and all the next day after the prom."

"All night!" her father's tone was thunderous. "I heard some talk about that business at the Rotary luncheon last week. I sat between Ben March and Ed Blair and it seems both their daughters are planning on it. Ben and Ed were pretty dubious, but their attitude seemed to be that if the other kids were doing it, then it must be all right. But I don't look at it that way. It used to be just the prom. Then it was the prom with a night club afterward. Now kids want to go driving around all night and go on to a picnic or something of the sort the next day with no sleep at all. It's ridiculous! But some parents seem afraid to take a firm stand."

When Dad ran out of breath, Mom said more mildly, but nonetheless firmly, "I think the whole idea's a mistake. It's not that we don't trust you, dear, but there's danger involved in those boys driving around for hours

on end. It's just asking for trouble—" she broke off, noticing the little smile playing around Marcy's mouth.
"You're not serious, are you?" she asked then.

"I said I was *supposed* to ask you about it," Marcy
reminded. "The thing is, I told Bruce I would. But—
I'm not very keen on the idea myself. I think it's kind of
crazy."

"That's exactly the word for it," Dad agreed, "crazy."

"I knew you'd feel that way," Marcy admitted, "but
—" she sighed, "it's all pretty complicated. I don't want
to stay out all night myself, but Bruce just takes it for
granted that's what you do on prom night. So if I say
I won't—well, I'll have to tell him he's free to ask someone else, if he wants to. And I already told Rick to ask
someone else, because I figured I'd be going with Bruce.
And if he already has—and if Bruce decides to—" her
voice ran down miserably.

She saw Mom's troubled glance meet Dad's equally
disturbed one. It wasn't necessary to come right out and
put the sorry fact into words. They both knew she'd be
left high and dry again, with no date for the prom at all.
And Marcy knew it. She knew it only too well. But she
also knew what she was going to do. There wasn't any
choice really. She'd never been one to go along with the
crowd, to do as the others did, even though her own
conscience warned her against it. Mr. Tuttle, in his
old-fashioned way, used to call it "having the courage of
your own convictions." Marcy could almost hear his
voice saying it. And there would be a little note of pride
in his tone, she thought, because Mr. Tuttle would approve of her decision. Just as her parents would approve

of it and as she approved herself, in spite of the ache of misery that went along with it.

"Bruce is going to stop by this afternoon," Marcy told Mom and Dad. "I said I'd know by then, although I guess I really knew last night, only I couldn't quite bring myself to come right out and say it. He'll think I'm such a square."

"Square," Mom said softly, her eyes proud on Marcy's face, "used to be a term of commendation. A person was called square if he was honest and fair and straight thinking."

"That won't be what Bruce means," Marcy said dryly.

"Are you sure," Dad asked, "that he won't want to take you to the prom, even if you can't stay out all night? Surely he'd consider your wishes in the matter."

Marcy shook her head. "It would spoil the whole thing for him. He thinks the only thing to do is go along with what his friends are planning. He's been looking forward to prom night all year. Of course," her voice choked a little, "I'll leave it up to him. But I have an idea I won't be needing that new white formal we were discussing, after all."

Her estimate of Bruce's reaction proved quite correct. "You mean," he asked, "you can't do it, or you won't? I don't believe you even tried to persuade your parents."

They were sitting in the little yellow car on the Rhodes' drive. Marcy had wasted no time in telling him of her decision and now Bruce's hands dropped away from the wheel and he stared at her narrowly, angrily.

Marcy said frankly, "I didn't try, really. Because I don't like the idea of it myself, Bruce."

"But, why?" he demanded. "Everybody else'll be out having fun. And we're not planning anything wrong, for creep's sake! Kids all over the country are having big all-night deals after their proms."

"Not nearly all of them," Marcy argued. "You say 'everybody' does it because it's what you want to do. But I look at it differently and there are lots of others like me."

"But you're spoiling my fun, too," Bruce's jaw jutted belligerently.

Marcy shook her head. "No, I'm not, Bruce. Because I'm not going to hold you to your invitation. You can ask another girl, one who'll celebrate prom night any way you like. Isn't that fair enough?"

Bruce stared at her. "You don't have to do that," he said, his tone a mixture of hope and uncertainty.

Marcy smiled, nodding. "I think that would be better all around. It's—just one of those things."

"But, gee, Marcy—I'd feel kind of funny going with someone else after I asked you."

"No need to," Marcy told him. "I guess we just weren't thinking about the same thing when you asked me to the prom and I accepted."

His glance was troubled. With an effort Marcy kept smiling.

"No hard feelings?" Bruce asked.

She shook her head. And to prove she meant it, she went for a little ride with him and, at his suggestion, stopped for a soda at the Sweet Shop. But when she waved good-bye to him a little later, Marcy had the feeling she wouldn't be seeing much of Bruce any more. She was faintly surprised at how little that seemed to matter. It was only the thought of missing out on the prom that hung heavily over her.

But when she'd had time to think things over, the conviction grew in Marcy that the sensible solution was to call Rick and tell him what had happened. There was such a good chance he hadn't asked anyone else yet. And she had no qualms of false pride or embarrassment about admitting her predicament to Rick. Not when they were so close and understood each other so well.

Mom, too, when Marcy broached the matter, agreed that this was the thing to do. "After all," she smiled, "he learned to dance just so he could take you. It wouldn't be fair not to let him know that the situation's changed now."

It was early evening by the time Marcy had reached a decision and gave the operator the Whitneys' number. Rick's sister answered and Marcy asked, "Bev, is Rick home? It's Marcy."

"Marcy?" a note of surprise came clearly over the wire. "I thought he was out with you. He had a date with some girl and I supposed—" she broke off, obviously embarrassed.

"That's okay," Marcy said. "It—wasn't important."

She was proud of how casual she sounded, when she felt as though the bottom had just dropped out of everything.

19

LET IT RAIN

MARCY had made an excuse to go up to her room quite early that evening; she had said she had homework to do. Parents never objected when you went off alone to do your school work. Without that explanation, Marcy knew hers might have felt she was going off to brood. And they would have tried to talk her into a game of some sort, or into having a cup of hot chocolate, anything to cheer her up. Marcy's lips curved in a faint indulgent smile at the thought. She was really very fond of her parents. But there were times when a person just had to be alone.

She did have a little homework, so she hadn't actually been fibbing. She got it out of the way first of all. Now she sat at her desk, her books still spread out around her, thinking. It was really in order to think that she had left her parents' cheerful company down in the living room. She had, she felt, quite a lot of thinking to do. There were some important and rather confusing matters to figure out.

Rick, Marcy listed mentally, and Bruce and the prom. It was really silly, she knew, to keep on thinking about the prom when she didn't have the slightest chance of getting to go to it. But it still lurked there in the back of her mind, casting its shadows of disappointment and regret. Still, she wasn't sorry that she wouldn't be going with Bruce. She was just achingly miserable because she couldn't go with Rick.

But you can't, Marcy reminded herself sternly. You know if he had a date with another girl tonight—the first girl he's ever taken out besides you, then it was for the purpose of inviting her to the prom. That's quite clear.

The thing that surprised her was that it should hurt so. And not just because of the prom. Marcy was baffled by the heat of her own feelings over the mere fact that Rick had a date with another girl at all! The sad and simple truth was that she was jealous!

She had let Bruce go without a quiver. Marcy was pretty sure she knew why. Bruce's attraction for her had always been based to a considerable extent on the fact that he was so good-looking and popular, that it was such a prideful thing merely to be seen with him and know that all the other girls were envious and impressed. But she had never been stirred by his kiss, not the way Rick's first awkward kiss had made her feel warmly happy and alive.

How, Marcy asked herself, could your relationship with a boy start out quite casually, without any of the fireworks and excitement generally associated with falling in love, and then develop, so slowly and unobtrusively that you scarcely noticed, into something rich and deep and real? Because that was the way she felt about Rick now. The mere thought of him was exciting, his slow grin, the way his hair fell across his forehead, the steadiness of his hazel eyes. And yet he was the same

Rick, different in no slightest degree, from the boy she had considered just a friend a while ago.

When had things changed between them, Marcy wondered, thinking back? Was it the winter day they had gone skating on the frozen river and she had brushed an imaginary speck of soot from Rick's nose, as an excuse for staring at him? Was it the time they had been caught in the big, echoing barn by the sudden rain and Rick's arms had felt so strong and good carrying her across the puddle? It had happened before the night of their first kiss, Marcy was sure of that. It had been building up quietly for a long time. It must have been, or she couldn't have felt such a lurch of disappointment, hearing Bev's thoughtless voice saying, "He had a date with some girl, and I supposed it was you."

So all right, Marcy thought, angry at the depth of her own feelings. He has a right to date other girls. You told him yourself to ask someone to the prom. You haven't any right to hold it against him.

She sighed. Thinking didn't seem to do much good after all. She got up and put a couple of records on her portable player, sentimental type records, and began getting ready for bed. She was just buttoning her pajamas when she heard a light knock on the door. At Marcy's, "Hi," her mother came in, bearing a steaming cup of hot chocolate with a couple of plump marshmallows melting on top.

"Ready for bed so soon?" Mom asked. "Dad and I were having some of this and thought you might like a cup, too."

Marcy thanked her and perched on the foot of her

bed to drink it. Her mother sat down on the dressing-table bench.

"Homework all finished?" she asked.

Marcy nodded. "I didn't have a lot," she admitted. "I really wanted to think about some things, too."

Her mother said hopefully, "Maybe Rick still hasn't asked another girl, honey. You can't be sure."

"I'm afraid he has," Marcy said. She took a sip of her drink, savoring its warm sweetness. "That wasn't all I had on my mind, though. I've been thinking a lot more about Rick than I have about the prom. I guess I've been growing fonder of him than I realized."

"It sometimes happens that way," her mother said quietly.

"Does it?" Marcy's voice held a note of surprise. "The thing is, in movies and stories and all—well, two people meet and—boom! It's a big thing between them. But with Rick, I wasn't very attracted to him at first. I never thought of our being any more than friends. Even now, I don't know when things changed, or why exactly. But I—I feel so different."

"It's like that quite often in real life," Mom said. "And feelings that grow slowly usually have deeper roots than the all-of-a-sudden sort of attraction. You see, there's so much more to being really fond of someone than just his first impact on you. There's liking and respect and mutual consideration, the knowledge that you can depend on one another. You can't find out about things like that right away."

Marcy nodded. "That's exactly how I feel about

Rick. And he said the other night that he wanted me to be happy more than anything in the world."

"Then I guess he feels the same way about you." Mom's smile was gentle. "And I don't think you need worry about his date with another girl changing that, even if he does ask her to the prom."

Marcy smiled, too. "That's just what I've been deciding," she admitted.

But deep inside, the thought of missing the prom still ached dully. Nor could she escape it all the next day. Despite the busy routine of classes, the necessity of staying after school to work on the paper, the little ache remained. When Marcy encountered Bruce casually in the hall between classes, he seemed rather more friendly than she had expected under the circumstances. Rick she didn't see at all except in study hall. And then he was deep in conversation with another boy as they left the room and only waved cheerfully at Marcy in passing. There was nothing at all unusual about this. It didn't have a thing to do with his date last night, she told herself firmly. Yet she felt disappointed just the same.

Up in the journalism room, she threw herself into editing a feature article on the mixed emotions of the graduating seniors, glad to linger for a while in the pleasant company of Jen and Howie and the others. She truly enjoyed her work on the *Breeze* and the opportunity it had afforded for warm friendships with the other staff members. And she had learned so much about the importance of teamwork and shared responsibility and the necessity of never letting the others down. Miss McCollum, Marcy felt, had done her a real favor when she asked her to take on the job of feature editor.

"Look!" Jen exclaimed, passing near the window as they were all getting ready to leave. "It's pouring!"

"Oh, fine," Marcy said. "It would hold off till now!"

"Anybody needs a lift," Howie told them, "wait at the front door. I'll bring my heap around from the parking lot."

They separated to go to their lockers. Marcy was the first one to reach the entrance. She pulled the hood of her raincoat up as she went through the door and out into the rainy dusk. Then she stopped, staring at the street.

Exactly as had happened once before, two cars awaited her. A small yellow one and an old battered green one. Marcy's heart quickened with delight as she caught Rick's eye and waved. Then, because it would have been inconsiderate not to, she waved at Bruce as well and called out in passing, "Sorry. Thanks for waiting. But I'm going with Rick."

She had a glimpse of his brows, lifting in surprise. Then she had reached the open door of Rick's car and was climbing in, to relax, smiling and a bit breathless against the worn cushions.

"He'll be sore," Rick said, a grin tugging at the corners of his mouth.

"Oh, well," Marcy shrugged. "I couldn't go with both of you, so I chose the one I'd rather go with."

"Thanks."

"You're welcome."

They both laughed, as though at some very witty remark. Bruce's car went splashing off through the rain. But Marcy didn't care. She couldn't imagine why he'd bothered to wait for her. But what did it matter? She dismissed the thought of Bruce airily. She was where she wanted to be, where she belonged. Here in Rick's old car, with his shoulder solid against hers, she felt warm and happy and glad to be alive. He reached out and turned on the ignition and the motor roared as they pulled away from the curb.

"Bev said you called last night," Rick told Marcy. Then, a trifle doggedly, "I took Nancy Corbett to the movies."

"You don't have to explain," Marcy smiled at him. "You can certainly date any girl you want to. It's okay." But why did he have to choose such a cute girl as Nancy?

"I didn't want to much," Rick said. "But you made me promise. And it seemed kind of queer just to ask her to the prom without ever having taken her out, so—"

"It's okay," Marcy said again, her smile beginning to quiver a little at the edges.

"Marcy," there was a note of desperation in his voice, "she's already going to the prom. And you have to let me out of that promise. I'm not going to keep on asking girls until—"

"Rick," Marcy reached out to lay her hand on his, "you don't have to ask a single other girl."

"I don't?"

Marcy shook her head. Her eyes were shining. She had never felt happier in her life. "I'm going with you."

"But—Bruce—?"

"That's all off now," Marcy told him. "And you know what? I'm glad it is. Because I'd rather go to the prom with you than anyone else in the world. So—unless you've changed your mind—"

"Gee!" Rick said. But his tone was so delighted, his grin so wide, the glow in his eyes so revealing, that further words weren't necessary.

Why was it, Marcy wondered, that such heavenly things always seemed to happen to her on rainy days?

20

PROM NIGHT

AS MARCY and Rick, with Liz and Hank trailing closely behind them, came into the country club ballroom on prom night, Marcy stopped quite still for a moment and stood staring. She couldn't help it. Everything seemed so different than it had that morning, when the decorating committee had swarmed about the place like beavers getting it all ready. Now, with the softly colored lights lending glamour and the orchestra playing and girls in varicolored dresses moving about, set off by the stark black and white of the boys' clothes, a new enchantment seemed to have settled over the familiar place.

"Boy, you really fixed it up," Rick said admiringly.

"Didn't we, though?" Marcy smiled up at him. "It looks much better than it did by daylight."

Liz cracked, "If they had the lights much dimmer, we couldn't find our way around."

"Hush, woman," Hank told her. "That's the way lights are supposed to be at proms. Dark and romantic." He held out his arms to Liz. "Shall we take the plunge?"

Liz nodded and they moved out onto the already crowded floor. But Marcy and Rick stood for a moment, just smiling at each other.

She thought he looked so nice in his white dinner

jacket and dark trousers, a deep red carnation in his but-
tonhole. Even the fact that the sleeves of the rented
coat were just a trifle short seemed curiously endearing
to Marcy. She tucked her hand through his arm. "Isn't
it fun!"

"Sure is," he agreed. His glance at her was proud and
impressed. "Gee, you look beautiful," he said simply.

Marcy glowed with pleasure, her eyes dropping to her
white organza dress, with its artfully fashioned strapless
bodice and wide ballerina skirt. It was as perfect a setting as she had dreamed of for the garnet necklace and
bracelet Mr. Tuttle had given her. The stones glowed
with deep red fire against her skin. And Rick's corsage
of dark red roses went perfectly with them. "Thanks,"
Marcy murmured. "I think it's a pretty dress, too."

"Not just the dress," Rick said and his elbow squeezed
her hand closer against his side. "Shall we dance?"

It was the beginning of an absolutely perfect evening.
Marcy couldn't remember ever having had more fun at
a dance. Maybe this was because it was Rick's first one
and his unjaded enjoyment enhanced her own. Or it
could have been the fact that she'd had a part in planning and carrying out the decorations. All the hopes and
fears that had preceded it, added to her awareness that
this would be her last high school dance, may have
sharpened her perceptions, too. But whatever the cause
it was a purely wonderful occasion.

Marcy saw Bruce dancing with his date, the strikingly
lovely Bett Kinley, who, it was rumored around school
had kept several boys dangling until she decided which
one she'd permit to take her to the prom. Bruce had

been the dark horse who entered the race late and out-distanced the others easily. But Marcy felt no slightest qualm of regret. She was perfectly happy with the way things had turned out.

Bruce and Bett and some of the others left quite early, soon after Sherry Clark had been crowned queen. But Marcy and Rick and Liz and Hank along with a good many others, stayed much later, enjoying the prom even more when the crowd had thinned a bit, which made for better dancing. Then the four of them drove in Hank's car to Clay City, where they had reservations at the Star-light Room. Eating supper and enjoying an excellent floorshow, they saw quite a few other couples they knew and it was all very gay and enjoyable.

Driving back toward Westfield, Marcy said, yawning, her head resting comfortably on Rick's shoulder, "I'm getting sleepy. What time is it?"

"Nearly two," Rick told her.

"But be sure to set the old alarm clock when you get home," Hank warned from the front seat. "We're pick-ing you and Liz up again at eight. And if you're not all set to head for the sand dunes by that time, it'll be just too bad."

"Don't worry," Liz said. "A few hours shut-eye will make new women of us, won't it, Marce?"

"Who wants *new* women?" Rick asked drolly.

Later, getting ready for bed, with the memory of Rick's kiss warm and exciting in her thoughts, Marcy was fumbling with the zipper of her dress when she heard the soft pad of Mom's slippered feet coming down the hall.

"Let me help," Mom murmured softly, a little smile curving her mouth. "I heard the car door shut and I couldn't resist coming in to find out how it all was."

"Wonderful," Marcy said dreamily. "Perfectly wonderful, every last minute of it. And I think Rick felt the same."

"I'll bet he did," Mom said, as she took the dress Marcy had just slipped out of and hung it in the closet. "Go to bed quickly and get some sleep. Your picnic lunch is all packed and ready. Dad and I probably won't be up when you leave, but have a nice time at the dunes. I listened to a late weather broadcast and it said clear and warm."

"That's what I call co-operation," Marcy yawned. She pulled on her pajamas and creamed her face automatically.

Mom gave her a little hug and headed her toward the bed. "You're half asleep already. I'll turn out your light. Good night, honey. . . ."

It was amazing what a few hours sleep could do for you. By the time the others came for her in the morning, Marcy was alert and ready to get going. In blue jeans and yellow jacket, a scarf tied around her hair, she answered Rick's discreet knock at the door with a cheerful, "Hi! Bet you thought I wouldn't be ready."

"We had to wait ten minutes for Liz." Rick grinned. "Here, let me take the food."

He took the brown paper bag from her and they went down the steps and out into the clear sunny morning. Today they were using Rick's car and as Marcy slid in and Rick climbed in beside her and started the motor, Liz said, "Sand dunes, here we come."

Hank, who had an excellent baritone voice started singing, "Off we go, into the wild blue yonder—" and they all joined in.

They sang and talked and laughed away the miles as they made the almost-three-hour-trip to the shore of Lake Michigan. Marcy loved the dunes with their wild untamed beauty, great hills of sand edging the level beach, with the tough wiry trees and grasses fighting for life and a foothold on their shifting sides. Rick parked the car near the edge of the park and the four of them walked the rest of the way, slipping and sliding, laughing and rough-housing, till they found a likely spot to spread their blankets and establish their picnic headquarters. The lake stretched in a blue expanse as far as the eye could see, the little breakers roaring and swishing as they licked the shore. The day was crystal clear and pleasantly warm for May, although the water was icy cold as they discovered when they took off their shoes and tested it.

"Some dim-brains are planning to swim," Liz said, retreating hastily as a wave swirled around her ankles.

"Bet they change their minds when they've had a sample," Rick chuckled.

"Let's walk up the beach and explore," Marcy said. And the others agreed readily.

They walked and climbed sand hills and slid down them. They skipped stones across the water and found curious bits and pieces of driftwood that intrigued the imagination. They met several people they knew, other couples who were following the prom with the traditional day of picnicking at the dunes. Some of them hadn't yet been home and were beginning to look washed-out and hollow-eyed. Others, like Marcy and Liz and Rick and Hank, had taken time out for a few hours sleep and were enjoying themselves more thoroughly. They didn't encounter Bruce and his foursome, but Marcy wasn't too surprised. After all, the sand dunes were pretty far-reaching.

By early afternoon, the four of them were ravenously hungry. They gathered driftwood, bleached silver-white and dry, and the boys built a fire near their picnic spot. They ate the chicken and ham sandwiches that Marcy's mother had made for them and the potato salad and relishes and cake Liz had brought along. Their lukewarm pop tasted delicious and they finished off with toasted marshmallows. Hank's little portable radio supplied them with music. And they talked about everything under the sun. Graduation and college and the future, funny things that had happened during their school years, the state of the world. Some serious talk, some humorous, sparked with laughter, with clowning, with kisses. A typical picnic, but a wonderful one, Marcy thought. Spending the whole long relaxing day with Rick seemed to add to the closeness and understanding that was growing between them at such a miraculous pace.

And she reflected, sitting there on the sandy blanket, with Rick's arm comfortably around her and her head leaning against his shoulder, how strangely things sometimes turned out. A feeling could grow and deepen. A second choice could become a first one. An association embarked upon quite casually could assume such importance in your life that it outshone other friendships like the sun dimming the light of a flickering candle. That was the way it was with Rick and her. And the knowledge was a warmth wrapping Marcy about, an answer to so many doubts and questions and uncertainties that had troubled her before.

All of them felt a real regret when the lengthening shadows warned them it was time to start for home. Rick told Marcy, his voice soft in her ear, "This is the kind of day that should never have to end."

Marcy nodded. "It's one I won't forget."

The trip home was just as enjoyable, but rather more quiet, than the one to the dunes had been. As they drew near Westfield, Rick announced that he was hungry and asked if the others wouldn't like to stop somewhere for something to eat.

"Ask a silly question, you get a silly answer," Hank said. "Of course we would! But what can we get that's cheap and filling? My finances are running low."

"How about pizza?" Marcy suggested, as she glimpsed TONY'S colorful neon sign a little way ahead.

"Perfect!" Liz agreed and both boys nodded.

They all looked a bit disheveled, walking into TONY'S in blue jeans and with faces beginning to glow with wind-burn. But there were other couples there from high school, equally pink and informally garbed, apparently winding up their prom week end in like manner. They greeted acquaintances on all sides as they made their way to a table.

The waitress who brought their menus gave Marcy a smile of recognition and said, "Hi." Then, as Marcy answered, she frowned and asked, "Say, have you heard about the accident?"

"Why, no," Marcy shook her head.

And Liz asked, "What accident?" as they all sat looking up inquiringly.

"Four of the kids from high school," the girl explained. "All in the hospital, but they're lucky to be alive. You know the driver," she nodded toward Marcy. "Good-looking blond fellow, I forget his name. Drives a little yellow convertible."

"What happened?" the question came in a sort of chorus. Marcy felt a queer, sinking sensation in her stomach.

"He must have gone to sleep at the wheel, they say. The car turned over in a ditch—it's a real mess." The waitress shook her head. "One of the girls got a concussion and they all have some broken bones. But it could be worse."

There was a flurry of questions and exclamations from the others, but for a moment Marcy couldn't say a word. Horror and pity stopped her throat. What a way for the prom to end! It was so dreadful and she might well have been a part of it, if she hadn't turned Bruce down and gone with Rick instead. The knowledge made Marcy shiver.

Perhaps the same thought had occurred to Rick, because Marcy felt his hand close around hers under the sheltering edge of the table. And she clung to it, feeling warmth and strength flow back along her nerves again, pushing away the blackness of that first shocked moment of realization.

Her eyes met Rick's and her look told him so many things. Things she'd have plenty of time for putting into words later.

THE END

4496